PENNY JORDAN

The Perfect Lover

THE CRIGHTONS

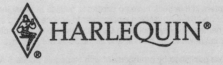

HARLEQUIN®

TORONTO • NEW YORK • LONDON
AMSTERDAM • PARIS • SYDNEY • HAMBURG
STOCKHOLM • ATHENS • TOKYO • MILAN • MADRID
PRAGUE • WARSAW • BUDAPEST • AUCKLAND

ISBN 0-373-12025-7

THE PERFECT LOVER

First North American Publication 1999.

This was what she had ached for...

She had been *so* hungry for him to kiss her like this, she acknowledged dizzily, as his mouth started to move over hers. She adjusted her body to get closer to him and felt him shift his weight to accommodate her.

Against his mouth she cried his name....

"Saul. Saul...Saul...."

Abruptly Louise found herself being set free, *pushed* away from the intimacy of the male body her own craved so badly. Only his hands still held her.

"Open your eyes, Louise," she heard a harsh and shockingly familiar male voice demanding bitingly. "I am *not* your precious Saul, whoever he might be...."

Dear Reader,

THE CRIGHTONS

The response to Penny Jordan's dramatic series of books about the turbulent lives of the Crighton family has been overwhelming, with many readers writing in to say that they have become so involved with the characters that they feel "part of the family."

Penny Jordan continues her family saga with **The Perfect Lover**, and it's the turn of Louise Crighton to find personal happiness. After the disastrous outcome of her crush on her cousin Saul, she can just about bring herself to face her family again. But how will she cope working with Gareth Simmonds, the man whose arms once offered more than just comfort and support?

All of the books featuring the Crighton family can be read in isolation, as each tells its own fascinating story, but if you wish to read the whole collection, then these are the novels to look for:

The Crighton Family

Haslewich branch of the family

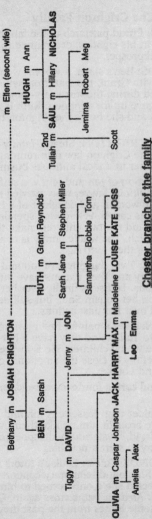

m Ellen (second wife)

Bethany m **JOSIAH CRIGHTON**

HUGH m Ann

SAUL m Hillary **NICHOLAS**

Jemima Robert Meg

2nd
Tullah m

Scott

BEN m Sarah

RUTH m Grant Reynolds

Sarah Jane m Stephen Miller

Samantha Bobbie Tom

Jenny m **JON**

MAX m Madeleine **LOUISE KATE JOSS**

Leo Emma

Tiggy m **DAVID**

OLIVIA m Caspar Johnson **JACK HARRY**

Amelia Alex

Chester branch of the family

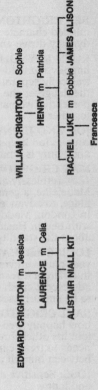

EDWARD CRIGHTON m Jessica

WILLIAM CRIGHTON m Sophie

LAURENCE m Celia

HENRY m Patricia

ALISTAIR NIALL **KIT**

RACHEL LUKE m Bobbie **JAMES ALISON**

Francesca

The Crighton Family

BEN CRIGHTON: Proud patriarch of the family, a strong-minded character in his eighties, determined to see his dynasty thrive and prosper.

RUTH REYNOLDS: Ben's sister, a vibrant woman now happily reunited with Grant, the man from whom she was tragically separated during the war years—and also with the daughter she gave up for adoption. Ruth is a caring, perceptive woman and she holds the Crighton family together.

JON AND JENNY CRIGHTON: Steady, family-oriented couple. Jon keeps the Crighton law firm running smoothly, and Jenny is a partner in a local antiques business.

MAX CRIGHTON: Son of Jon and Jenny, a self-assured, sexy, ruthlessly ambitious lawyer who married his wife, Madeleine, a gentle woman and daughter of a High Court judge, to advance his career. While Max spends the week in London, Maddy and the two children make their home with Ben in Haslewich. The whole family is concerned about the stability of their marriage.

LOUISE and KATE: Twin daughters of Jon and Jenny. A year out of university and their careers have pulled them in different directions. Louise is finally over her adolescent crush on her cousin Saul, but still has reason to be embarrassed over her past actions.

SAUL CRIGHTON: After a painful first marriage, he is now happily wed to Tullah and they have a baby son to join his other three young children. He is aware that he needs to tread carefully to close the emotional gap between himself and Louise.

JOSS: Sensitive and caring fourteen-year-old son of Jon and Jenny.

JACK: Two years older than Joss, he is Jon and Jenny's nephew. They have brought him up like their own son since his father, David, mysteriously disappeared and his mother moved away to start a new life.

GARETH SIMMONDS: One of Louise's tutors while she was at university. She found temporary comfort in his arms, but he suspected she'd only turned to him as a substitute for Saul. As their paths cross again, Gareth knows they have some issues from the past they need to resolve.

CHAPTER ONE

'MY GOODNESS, we *are* honoured, aren't we? It isn't very often these days that you manage to tear yourself away from the bureaucratic delights of Brussels.'

Louise tensed as she heard the sarcastic voice of her elder brother, Max. They had never got on particularly well, even as children, and in her view maturity had done nothing to improve either their relationship or her brother.

'It was commented at Christmas that you weren't around,' Max continued jibingly. 'But, of course, we all know Saul was really the reason for that, don't we?'

Louise gave him an angry look before retorting, 'Perhaps if you spent more time thinking about your own relationships and less talking about other people's you might learn something genuinely worthwhile, but then you never were much good at appreciating what's really of value in this life, were you, Max?'

Without giving him any opportunity to retaliate, Louise turned on her heel and walked quickly away from him.

She had promised herself that on this, her first visit home since she had started working in Brussels over twelve months ago, she would prove to her family just how much she had changed...matured...and just how different, distant almost, she was from the girl who...

Out of the corner of her eye she caught sight of

Saul, her father's cousin, who was standing with his
wife, Tullah, and the three children from his first marriage. Tullah had her arm around Megan, Saul's
daughter, while Saul held the little boy they had had
together.

The large drawing room of her grandfather's house
seemed to be filled by the presence of her peers,
proudly showing off their growing families.

Clustered around the fireplace were her cousin
Olivia, with her husband and their two children, talking animatedly with Luke, from the Chester branch of
the family, and his American wife Bobbie and their
little girl, while Maddy, her brother Max's wife, kept
a discreet eye on Gramps, who was becoming increasingly irascible.

According to her mother, Maddy was close to a
saint for humouring him the way she did. When Jenny
Crighton had made this comment this morning, over
breakfast, Louise had immediately pointed out that if
Maddy could put up with being married to Max, then
her grandfather must come as a form of light relief.

'Louise,' her mother had protested, but Louise had
remained unrepentant.

It was no secret in the family that Max was not a
good or kind husband to Maddy, and privately Louise
couldn't understand why on earth Maddy stayed with
him.

'You're looking very cross.'

Louise grimaced as she saw her twin sister. Twins
were a feature of the Crighton family, in the same
way that poppies were a feature of a field of corn—
they sprang up all over the place, although as yet there
were no sets in the current new generation.

'They'll come,' her father's aunt Ruth had predicted.

'I've just been receiving the benefit of Max's brotherly conversation,' Louise informed her grimly. 'He doesn't change…'

'No…' Katie looked at her twin. 'You know, in a lot of ways I feel quite sorry for him. He—'

'*Sorry* for *Max*?' Louise exploded. 'What on earth for? He's got everything he's ever wanted—a cushy place in one of the country's leading sets of chambers, with his pick of all the best briefs—and all he's had to do to get it is to persuade poor Maddy to marry him.'

'Yes, I know what he's got in the material sense, Lou, but is he happy?' Katie persisted. 'I think he feels what happened with Uncle David far, far more than he's ever shown. After all, they—'

'They were both made in the same mould. Yes, I know,' Louise cut in. 'If you want my opinion, it would be a good thing for this family if Uncle David *never* surfaced again. Olivia as good as told me that her father had been guilty of serious malpractice when he and Dad were partners, and that if he hadn't disappeared when he did…'

Both of them were silent for a moment as they remembered David Crighton, their father's twin brother and Olivia's father, and the near disaster he had plunged the family into prior to his disappearance some years earlier.

'That's all in the past now,' Katie reminded her gently. 'Dad and Olivia have managed to sort out all the problems they had been having with the practice—and in fact they've built up the business so much that they've decided they need to think about

taking on an extra qualified solicitor to cope with the
increased workload. But Gramps still misses David,
you know. He was always—'

'The favourite. Yes, I know. Poor Gramps. He
never has had very good judgement, has he? First he
makes David the favourite, ahead of Dad, and now
it's Max.'

'Mum's really glad that you were able to make it
home for Gramps's birthday,' Katie told her sister
quietly. 'She was…upset at Christmas when you
didn't come home…'

'When I *couldn't* come home,' Louise corrected her
sharply. 'I told you at the time. My boss put me under
pressure to put together a report on the legal aspects
of a new community law she thought might be passed,
and I had no option but to agree. It wouldn't have
been worth coming home for what would have
amounted to just about forty-eight hours, even if I
could have got the flights.'

Three months after leaving university, and not
wanting to take the next stage in her training to become a barrister immediately, Louise had taken a temporary post working for a newly appointed Euro MP
who'd wanted someone to work for her as a legal
researcher.

Six months ago the temporary post had become a
permanent one, and while the hours were long and the
work extraordinarily demanding, Louise had thrown
herself into it with determination, knowing that the
contacts she was making in Brussels would ultimately
equip her to make a change of career should she want
to do so.

Their choice of careers couldn't have been more
different, Katie acknowledged as she silently and

sympathetically studied her twin. While Louise, true to her nature, had chosen to fling herself head-first into the maelstrom of politics and intrigues in the hot-house melting-pot atmosphere of Europe's bureau-cratic capital, she had opted to join a still very youth-ful and emergent new charity which had been set up to help young children across the world who had been made orphans and refugees by war.

'Have you spoken to Saul and Tullah yet?' Kate asked her sister softly.

Louise reacted sharply to her question, tensing and almost physically backing off from her as she replied angrily, 'No, I haven't…Why should I? For God's sake, *when* is everyone in this wretched family going to stop behaving as though…?' She stopped, and took a deep breath.

'Look, for the last time, Saul means nothing to me now. I had a silly, stupid crush on him, yes. I made a total and complete fool of myself over him, yes. But…' She stopped again, and shook her head.

'It's over, Katie. Over.'

'Mum thought when you didn't come home at Christmas—' Katie began.

Louise wouldn't let her finish, breaking in bitterly, 'That what? That I couldn't bear the thought of seeing Saul? Or, worse, that I might—'

'She thought that perhaps you'd met someone in Brussels.' Katie overrode her with quiet insistence. 'And that you weren't coming home because you wanted to be with him…'

Interestingly, a soft tide of warm colour started to tinge her sister's skin, and, even more interestingly, for once in her life she seemed almost lost for words as she turned her head and looked down at the carpet before saying quickly, 'No. No, there isn't anyone…at least not like that. I…'

It wasn't totally true—there was someone, of sorts—but she knew perfectly well that the relationship Jean Claude wanted with her was one based on sex only.

Jean Claude was twelve years older than her, and moved in the higher echelons of Brussels' diplomatic circles. He was, as he himself had told Louise, a career diplomat, who currently held a post connected with the French fishing industry.

Louise wasn't quite sure as yet how she felt about him. He had a suave, dry sense of humour, and the kind of Gallic good looks that fell just short enough of outrageously handsome to ensure that he was very attractive to the female sex. Politics and the law, as Jean Claude had already teasingly commented to her, could make very exciting bedfellows.

'Brazen, I think you mean,' Louise had corrected him firmly.

'Be careful if you're looking for commitment,' a colleague had already warned Louise. 'He's got a reputation for liking variety.'

Louise had shrugged away the other woman's comments. Commitment was the last thing on her mind at the moment, and would be for a very long time to come. She might be over Saul in the sense that she was no longer suffering from the massive crush which had caused her to make such an idiotic fool of herself, but she was certainly far from over the feelings of humiliation and searing self-disgust—self-dislike—which had resulted from the sharp realisation of just how dangerously and potentially destructively out of control her feelings for Saul had threatened to become.

She would certainly never make that mistake again. *Never* allow herself to become such a victim, such a slave to her emotions ever again—she didn't really understand how it had happened in the first place. Right from her early teens she had set her sights firmly on aiming for a career. Marriage, babies, emotions, although she'd once have openly welcomed them with Saul, were more Katie's forte than her own. The terrifying force of her feelings for Saul had been an abberation, and the behaviour they had resulted in so totally abhorrent and repugnant to her that even now, nearly three years later, she could scarcely bear to think about it.

Yes, it was possible now for her to look at Saul with Tullah and the children without suffering even the smallest flicker of the emotion which had torn her apart and threatened every aspect of her normal life during those months when it had held its strangulating, choking grip on her life. But what *wasn't* possible, what she suspected might *never* be possible, was for her to forget just how traumatic that time, those *feelings* had been.

Louise frowned, her thoughts switching from the past to the present as she recognised the suspiciously furtive way her younger brother Joss and their cousin Jack were edging their way towards the French windows.

Discreetly following them, she waited until Joss was on the point of unlatching the door before demanding sternly, 'And just where do the pair of you think you are going?'

'Lou…'

Considerably startled, her brother released his hold on the door handle and spun round to face her.

'We were just going down to the greenhouse,' Jack told her with virtuous innocence. 'Aunt Ruth is growing some special seeds there and...'

'The greenhouse?' Louise questioned loftily. 'This compelling expedition to view Aunt Ruth's seedlings wouldn't have been taken via the TV room, would it?'

The look of contrived injured innocence her brother gave her made Louise's lips twitch slightly, but Jack wasn't quite such a good actor, and his fair skin was already starting to flush with guilt. Both boys were ardent rugby fans, and Louise had overheard them pleading with her mother, without success, earlier in the day to be allowed to sneak away from the family party in order to watch their favourite game.

'The All Blacks are playing,' Joss told her pleadingly.

'You'll be all black, or rather your good behaviour record will be, if Mum catches on to what you're up to,' Louise warned him.

'If we go now, we can just about catch the last half,' Joss told her winningly. 'And Mum won't even notice. We'll be back before she knows we're gone.'

'I don't think...' Louise began, but Joss was already reaching up to give her a fervent hug.

'Thanks Lou, you're the best,' he announced. 'And if Mum should ask...'

Louise shook her head firmly.

'Oh, no...don't drag me in. If you get found out, you're on your own, the pair of you.' But she was smiling affectionately as she returned her brother's warm hug. After all, it wasn't such a very long time ago that she herself had found such family gatherings rather dull, and had, like Joss and Jack, made her escape from them just as quickly as she could.

'Bet you wish you could come with us,' Joss whispered to her with an engaging grin before quickly sliding through the French window.

'To watch the All Blacks? No, thanks,' Louise retorted with a small female shudder, but she was smiling as she discreetly closed the French windows behind the two boys.

On the other side of the room Tullah, who had been watching the scene, touched Saul on the arm.

As he turned to look at her she took their son out of his arms and told him, 'I'm just going to have a word with Louise.'

Frowning slightly, Saul watched her. She had totally transformed his life, and the lives of his three children from his first marriage.

Louise stiffened as she saw Tullah making her way towards her. She looked quickly over her shoulder, but the door from the drawing room was blocked by her father and Aunt Ruth, who were deep in conversation. Katie, whom she might have expected to be her ally, had somehow or other managed to melt away, and now there was no escape for her. Tullah was already at her side.

'Hello, Louise...'

'Tullah.'

'You've had your hair cut. I like it. It suits you...'

'Thank you.'

Automatically Louise touched one of the short feathery curls of her newly shorn hair. She had had her hair cut on impulse the day before she had flown home, and the feminine cut showed off the delicacy of her bone structure and emphasised the shape and colour of her dark eyes. The weight she had lost while away at university had never totally been replaced. She looked, Tullah acknowledged inwardly, almost a little too fine-boned and fragile, and she could well understand, as a mother herself, why Jenny should be a little bit anxious over her well-being.

As the silence between them stretched Louise was acutely conscious of the fact that virtually everyone else in the room was probably watching them and remembering...

As she turned to move away from Tullah, baby Scott reached out and, grinning winsomely at Louise, patted her cheek with one fat baby hand, pronouncing solemnly, 'Pretty.'

Over his downy head Tullah's sympathetic eyes met Louise's wary, startled ones.

'Oh, dear. I think I'm going to sneeze.' Tullah told Louise. 'Could you take him for me?'

Before Louise could protest she found herself holding a solid armful of gurgling, beaming baby, whilst Tullah dived into her jacket pocket for a tissue.

'No. No, it's gone...' Tullah announced when the threatened sneeze was not forthcoming, but she made no attempt to take her son back from Louise as she commented, 'It's so nice to see virtually all the family here. I know your grandfather isn't always the easiest person to get along with...'

'You can say that again,' Louise agreed wryly, gently detaching the baby's clutching fingers from the gold chain she was wearing around her neck. 'He's got your colouring but Saul's eyes,' she told Tullah. 'How have the other three...?'

'So far, so good,' Tullah told her, showing her her

crossed fingers. 'It's probably been easier for them, and for us in one way, because they live with us full time. So there's no question of them feeling that Scott, here, gets to see more of their father than they do.'

Scott, for some reason, had quite obviously taken an immediate liking to Louise, and much to her own astonishment, and Tullah's patent amusement, he started to press loud juicy kisses against her face.

Louise, despite her determination to focus on her career, had always liked children and enjoyed their company. As a teenager she had often babysat for Saul, and had formed quite a close bond with his three, and now, to her chagrin, she suddenly felt her eyes filling with emotional feminine tears as Scott's baby kisses touched her skin.

Quickly she handed him back to Tullah, telling her chokingly, 'Tullah, I'm sorry…'

And both of them knew that it wasn't what was happening now that she was apologising for.

Very gently Tullah touched her arm.

'It's over, Lou,' she told her softly. 'Forget it. We have. You were missed at Christmas—by all of us…' As she turned to return to Saul and the children, she paused and dropped a light kiss on Louise's cheek.

'Forget it', Tullah had said. Louise closed her eyes as Tullah walked away. If only she could. Tullah and Saul might have forgiven her, but she doubted that she would ever be able to forgive herself…

'Is everything all right, darling?'

Louise forced a determined smile as she read the concern in her mother's eyes.

'Fine,' she assured her. A quick look around her grandfather's drawing room reassured her that she was no longer the object of everyone's discreet attention. Taking a deep breath, Louise commented as steadily as she could, 'I was just saying to Tullah that Scott has Saul's eyes but her colouring...'

'Yes, he has, hasn't he?' Jenny Crighton agreed gratefully, relief leaking through the anxiety that had gripped her.

In one sense it had been a relief when Louise had finally agreed to come home for her grandfather's birthday, but in another...

Louise was her daughter, and she loved her, worried over her—how could she not do so?—but she had to admit that she had been anxious.

Louise had a quick temper coupled with a very easily bruised sense of pride. Watching Max talking with his sister earlier had made Jenny pray that Max wouldn't do or say something to upset his sister and put her on the defensive.

Tullah and Olivia—Jenny's niece and Louise's cousin—had both tried to reassure Jenny that everything would be all right, that teenage crushes were something that happened to everyone, and that it was just Louise's misfortune that hers had happened to be conducted under such a public glare of family attention, and that the object of her untrammelled teenage passion had been a member of her own family.

'She behaved so very badly,' Jenny had reminded them sorrowfully.

'Things did get a little out of hand,' Tullah had agreed. 'But since Louise's behaviour resulted in Saul and I getting together, and recognising how we really felt about one another far more quickly than we might otherwise have done, I have to admit that I feel more inclined to be grateful to her than anything else.'

'Louise made a mistake,' Olivia had added. 'Making mistakes is something we all do, and personally I think she'll end up a better, more well-rounded person for having had it brought home to her that she is fallible and human. She *was* rather inclined to think herself above everyone else,' she had reminded Jenny ruefully. 'A combination, perhaps, of a certain Crighton gene plus a very, very shrewd brain. What happened has softened her, made her realise that she's a human being and that there are some things she can't programme herself to achieve...'

'Have you had anything to eat yet?' Jenny pressed now. Jon, her husband, kept reminding her that Louise was now an adult woman, living her own life and holding down a very high-pressured job, but to Jenny she was still very much one of her babies, and to a mother's concerned eye Louise looked just that little bit too slender.

'I was just going to get myself something,' Louise fibbed. She was well aware of just how generous Tullah had been in coming over to her like that, but despite that generosity there was still a small knot of anxiety in Louise's stomach which made her feel that it would be unwise trying to eat.

'I was just on my way to wish Gramps a happy birthday,' she told her mother, and hopefully, once she had done so, she would be able to leave without the others thinking that...that what? That she was running away?

Running away. No, she wasn't doing that, had *never* done that, despite what some people chose to think!

'European Parliament...bunch of committee-making bureaucrats who are far too removed from what's going on in the real world...'

Louise gritted her teeth as she listened to Ben Crighton, her grandfather and family patriarch, a few minutes later. As she was perfectly well aware, so far as *he* was concerned the only real way, the only worthwhile way, to practise the law was from a barrister's chambers.

Excusing herself before she allowed him to provoke her into an argument, Louise couldn't help feeling sorry for Maddy, who had moved into the old man's large country house following an operation on his hip the year before.

The move, at first merely a temporary one to ensure that he had someone to care for him in the short term, had turned into a more permanent arrangement, with Maddy and the children living full time in Haslewich with Max's grandfather while Max spent most of his time living and working in London.

Louise couldn't understand how or why Maddy put up with Max's blatant selfishness—and his equally blatant infidelities. She certainly would never have done so, but then she would never have married a man like her brother in a thousand lifetimes. She knew how much it distressed her parents that he had turned out the way he had. Max was as unprincipled and selfish in other areas of his life as he was in his role as a husband.

Unlike their uncle David, Olivia's father and her own father's twin brother, Max might never have actually broken the law, but Louise suspected that he was perfectly capable if not of doing so, then certainly of bending it to suit his own purposes.

'He doesn't change, does he?' The rueful, familiar tones of Saul's voice coming from behind her caused

Louise to whirl round, her face a stiff mask of wariness as she watched him.

The last time she and Saul had spoken to each other had been when he had consigned her to Olivia's charge, having just made it clear to her that, far from returning her feelings for him, he would really prefer never to have to set eyes on her again.

Words spoken in the heat of the moment, perhaps, but they had left their mark, their scar upon her, not least because she knew how richly deserved his fury and rejection of her had been.

'I suppose at his age…' Louise began, and then shook her head and agreed huskily, 'No. No, he doesn't.'

Ridiculous for her, at twenty-two, to feel as uncomfortable and ill at ease as a guilty child, but nevertheless she did.

Whatever malign fate had decided to make Saul the object of her teenage fantasies and longings had long since upped sticks and decamped from her emotions. The man she saw standing in front of her might not have changed but she certainly had. The Saul she saw standing before her now was once again, thankfully, nothing more to her than another member of her family.

'Your mother says you're only paying a flying visit home this time.'

'Yes. Yes, that's right,' Louise agreed. 'Pam Carlisle, my boss, has been asked to sit on a new committee being set up to look into the problems caused by potential over-fishing in the seas off the Arctic. Obviously from the legal angle there's going to be a lot of research work involved, which I'll be involved in.'

'Mmm...sounds like a good breeding ground for potential future Euro politicians in the Crighton family,' Saul teased, but Louise shook her head.

'No. Definitely not,' she denied firmly. 'Politics isn't for me. I'm afraid I'm far too outspoken for a start,' she told him ruefully. 'And politics requires a great deal more finesse than I'll ever possess.'

'You're too hard on yourself,' Saul told her. 'In more ways than one,' he added meaningfully, forcing her to hold his gaze as he added quietly, 'It's time for us to make a fresh start, Lou. What happened happened, but it's in the past now...'

Before she could say anything he added, 'Tullah and I will be coming over to Brussels some time in the next few months on company business. It would be nice if we could meet up...go out for dinner together...'

Saul worked for Aarlston-Becker, a large multinational company whose European head office was based just outside Haslewich. He and Tullah had met when she had gone to work in the company's legal department under Saul.

Unable to do anything other than simply nod her head, Louise was stunned when Saul suddenly reached out and took her in his arms, holding her tightly in a cousinly hug as he told her gruffly, 'Friends again, Lou.'

'Friends,' she managed to agree chokily, fiercely blinking back her tears.

'And don't forget...write to me...'

Louise grimaced as she listened to Katie's firm command. 'Why on earth did you have to go and get yourself involved with some wretched charity outfit that can't even run to the expense of a fax machine?' she groaned.

'*You* tell *me*...but I do enjoy my job,' Katie pointed out.

They were saying goodbye at the airport, their mother having dropped them off on her way to a meeting of the charity she and their great-aunt Ruth had set up in their home town some years earlier.

'Sorry I can't see you off properly,' she had apologised as they climbed out of her small car.

'Don't worry about it, Mum; we understand,' Louise had consoled her.

'You could always come over to Brussels to see me, you know,' Louise told her twin abruptly now. 'I'll pay for the ticket, if that would help.'

Katie gave her a brief hug. She knew how difficult it was for her sister to admit that there were any chinks in her emotional armour, even to her twin. To the world at large, Louise always came across as the more independent one of the two of them, the leader. But in reality Katie believed that *she* was the one with the less sensitively acute emotions, even though she knew that Louise would have sharply denied such an allegation. Louise had always taken upon herself the role of the bigger, braver sister, but Katie knew that inside Louise was nowhere near as confident or as determinedly independent as others seemed to think.

Even their parents seemed to have been deceived by Louise's outward assumption of sturdy bravado, and consequently *she* was the one who was always treated that little bit more gently, the one for whom extra allowances were always made, Katie acknowledged. A fact which made her oddly protective of her sister.

'Oh, by the way, did you know that Professor Simmonds has been seconded to Brussels? Apparently he's been asked to head some committee on fishing rights in the North Sea,' Katie told her vaguely.

'What? No, I *didn't* know,' Louise responded, her face paling.

'No? I thought that perhaps you may have bumped into him,' Katie told her innocently.

'No, I haven't!' But if what Katie had just told her was true, Louise suspected that she was certainly going to do so. The committee Katie was talking about had to be the same one that Louise's boss had just been co-opted onto. Of all the unwanted coincidences!

Louise's thoughts rioted frantically, her stomach churning, but she dared not let Katie see how shocked and disturbed she was.

'I know you don't *like* him,' Katie was saying quietly.

'No. I don't,' Louise agreed curtly. 'After all, he cost me my first, and—'

'Louise, that's not fair,' Katie objected gently.

Louise looked away from her. There was so much that Katie didn't know, that she *couldn't* tell her.

Gareth Simmonds had been her tutor at Oxford at a particularly traumatic time in her life, and he had been a witness not just to that trauma, and the way she had made a complete and utter fool of herself, but he had also...

Louise bit her lip. The feeling of panic churning her stomach was increasing instead of easing.

'That's the final call for my flight,' she told Katie thankfully, giving her twin a swift hug before grabbing hold of her flight bag and heading for her gateway.

Gareth Simmonds in Brussels!

That was all she needed!

CHAPTER TWO

GARETH SIMMONDS in Brussels! Louise gave a small groan and closed her eyes, shaking her head in refusal of the stewardess's offer of a drink.

Trust Katie to wait to drop *that* bombshell on her until the last minute. Still, at least she *had* warned her, and forewarned was, as they say, forearmed.

Gareth Simmonds. She ground her teeth in impotent fury. She had been halfway through her first year when he had stepped into the shoes of her previous tutor, who'd had to retire unexpectedly on the grounds of ill health, and he and Louise had clashed right from the start.

She had resented the far more pro-active role he had made it plain he intended to play as her tutor. She had been used to his elderly and ailing predecessor, who had, in the main, been content to leave her to her own devices—something which had suited Louise down to the ground, giving her, as it had, ample opportunity to give the minimum amount of attention to her studies whilst she concentrated on what had become the far more important matter of making Saul fall in love with her.

The situation would have been bad enough if Gareth Simmonds had merely concerned himself with his official role as her tutor, but, no, that hadn't been enough for him. He had had the gall...the cheek...the...the effrontery to take it upon himself to interfere in her personal life as well.

25

Louise's tense shoulders twitched angrily. The last thing she needed right now—just when she was beginning to feel she was getting her life back on an even keel again, just when the events of the weekend had made her feel that at last, *finally*, she had begun to reclaim her sense of self-respect—was to have the whole ugly mess of her past dragged up again in the person of Gareth Simmonds.

He was going to Brussels to head a committee, Katie had said, when repeating to her the information she had garnered at an informal reunion of her old university classmates, and not just any committee either. Louise could feel her body starting to tense defensively. The thought that she might have to have any kind of contact with Gareth Simmonds was unacceptable, untenable. Anger, pride and panic started to well up inside her, causing her throat to tighten as though her own despairing emotions were threatening to choke her.

Gareth Simmonds. They had clashed straight away, something about him sending sharp, prickling, atavistic feelings of dislike and apprehension quivering through her body, and that had been *before* that disastrous confrontation between them at the end of her first year at Oxford, when he had sent for her and warned her of the potentially dire consequences of her not giving more time and attention to her work.

She had been far more headstrong and self-willed in those days, and the fact that he had had the gall to challenge her over anything, never mind the torment of her love for Saul, had driven her to retaliate. But he had been too quick for her, too subtle…too…

She had hated him with much the same intensity with which she had loved Saul, and with just as little effect, and the last thing she wanted or needed at this stage in her life was to be confronted with the physical evidence of her own youthful stupidity.

She could still remember...

There had been a good deal of giggling and gossip when he had first arrived at Oxford—the youngest Chair they had ever had, and the sexiest, according to his female students. Louise had shrugged her shoulders in disdain. *However* sexy *others* might find him, *she* was not interested. In her eyes he could never match up to Saul. No man could.

True, he might be over six feet with the kind of Celtic colouring that produced a lethal combination of thick dark hair and incredibly brilliant dark blue eyes, but for all Louise cared he could have modelled for the hunchback of Notre Dame.

'Have you *heard* his voice,' one besotted student had breathed, wild-eyed. 'I could orgasm just listening to him.'

Louise had looked witheringly at her. *Saul's* voice made her go weak at the knees, and Gareth Simmonds sounded nothing like him. In fact, the only things they did have in common were that they were both in their thirties—although Gareth Simmonds was a good seven years younger than Saul—and they could both display a decidedly brutal verbal toughness when they so chose. From Saul, the merest hint of a sharp word could reduce her to choking black misery. From Gareth Simmonds it tended to provoke a fierce desire to retaliate in kind.

He *might* have been her tutor, but that hadn't given him the right to interfere in her life in the way he had done—and besides... But, no, she must not think about that—not now.

Abruptly Louise realised that the plane had landed.

Automatically she stood up and reached to retrieve her bag from the overhead locker, and then froze as the man occupying the seat behind her also stood up to do the same thing.

'You!' she whispered as she came face to face with the very man who had just been occupying her thoughts and exercising her temper.

'Hello, Louise.' Gareth Simmonds acknowledged her calmly. Shakily Louise grabbed her bag and turned her back on him. What an appalling coincidence that *he* should be on the same flight as her!

Determinedly keeping her back towards him, Louise edged her way into the aisle and headed for the exit.

A sharp wind whipped across the tarmac as they left the plane, and as she hurried towards the arrivals lounge Louise reassured herself that her quickened pace was caused by the chilly evening air, and certainly not by any fear of coming face to face with Gareth Simmonds a second time.

Once through Customs Louise headed for the taxi rank, giving the cab driver her address at the large block of apartments where she lived. The apartment she rented was small, and fearsomely expensive, but at least she lived on her own, she comforted herself as she paid off the taxi driver and walked into the apartment block foyer.

While she filled the kettle, Louise ran her answering machine tape. A small rueful smile curled her mouth as she heard Jean Claude's familiar, sexy, smoky French accent. She had dated the Frenchman casually a few times, but was well aware of his reputation as an incorrigible flirt.

He was telephoning to ask if she was free for dinner during the week. Louise went to pick up and open her diary. She was due to accompany her boss to an inaugural meeting of the new committee in the morning. She suspected it might possibly run on until after lunch, and then at night there was an official dinner.

'The French contingent especially are going to be asking some tricky questions,' Pam Carlisle had warned Louise. 'They're none too happy about the fact that the Chair appointed is British. It's only the fact that he's known to be pro-European that's persuaded them to give their grudging acceptance of his appointment. The disputed waters are, after all, still officially British.'

'But they want to change that...' Louise had guessed.

'Well, they certainly want to get their own legal right to fish the waters.'

They had gone on to discuss the legal ramifications of the situation, and Louise had never thought to ask her boss the identity of the committee's Chair. Why should she have done? It had never even crossed her mind that the new appointee could possibly be her ex-tutor and protagonist Gareth Simmonds. Hadn't his prestigious lectureship coupled with the doting adoration of half the female student population been enough for him? Louise wondered bitterly.

'I'll bet he's absolutely heaven in bed,' she could remember one of her co-students breathing excitedly. 'And he's not married.'

'Heaven in bed'. Louise tensed abruptly. He had certainly been hell out of it! To her at least.

'He's rumbled us,' Katie had warned her. 'He's

guessed that I've been sitting in at lectures to cover for you. He actually *called* me Katherine yesterday…'

'So…?' Louise had said grittily. 'That *is* your name, isn't it?'

'It's *my* name,' Katie had agreed. 'But at the time I was attending one of his lectures pretending to be *you*.'

'He probably made a genuine mistake,' Louise had told her irritably. She had gone home to Haslewich, on the pretext of having left some of her books behind on her last visit home, but in reality so that she could see Saul. To her chagrin, though, Saul had been away on business, and the whole exercise had proved to be a complete waste of time.

In those days she had not always treated her twin as considerately as she might have, Louise acknowledged now, as the boiling kettle disturbed her reverie, and in fact it was probably very true to say she had often been guilty of bullying and browbeating Katie into doing as *she* wanted.

Things were different now, of course. She had done what she could to make amends, and, as she was the first to acknowledge, there were areas in which her twin had shown considerably more strength of purpose and determination than she could ever have exhibited herself.

She had been in her late teens then, though, and so totally obsessed with Saul that nothing else, *no one* else, had been important.

Briefly she closed her eyes. This afternoon, when Saul had put his arms round her to give her that firm fraternal hug, initially her body had totally recoiled from his touch—not out of rejection but out of fear, a deep-rooted, instinctive, self-protective fear that there might be some hidden part of her that was still susceptible to her old romantic dreams. But to her relief what she had actually felt, *all* she had actually felt, had been a warm and very reassuring sense of peace and release, coupled with the knowledge that there was nothing, after all, for her to fear. Being hugged by Saul, being held in his arms, had meant no more to her than if he had been Olivia's husband Caspar, or one of the Chester cousins, or indeed any other man of whom she had reason to be fond in a totally non-sexual and uncomplicated way.

She had *known* then that she was truly and totally free of the past, at least where *Saul* was concerned.

Frowningly she stirred her coffee.

She had behaved foolishly when she had been at university, there was no getting away from that fact, but she wasn't alone in having done that—many other students had done the same.

She picked up her coffee mug too quickly and some of the hot liquid spilled onto her hand. She cursed angrily under her breath.

Damn Gareth Simmonds. *Why* on earth couldn't he have stayed safely where he was in Oxford—and in her past?

The *last* thing she needed right now was having him around studying her...watching her with those too perceptive, too knowing evening-sky-blue eyes of his...judging her...just *waiting* for her to make a mistake...

Louise started to grind her teeth.

Well, she'd got news for him. She wasn't the Louise she had been at Oxford any longer. She was a *woman* now, an adult, holding down a highly responsible and demanding job, proving that she could control and run her *own* life, that she didn't need the constant back-up and support of her twin sister to be there at her side all the time, to do her bidding, to make her feel whole and complete. God, but she had hated him for throwing that accusation at her—just one of the scathing criticisms he had made of her!

It should have been *Saul's* denouncement of her, after she had so dangerously tricked Tullah into following her into the maze and left her there at the masked ball, that should have remained like a scar on her consciousness, a dialogue that ran for ever through her head as she tried to argue her way out of it, but oddly it wasn't. It was her arguments, her confrontations with her tutor about which she *still* had bad dreams, and still, in times of stress, played over and over again through her memory.

Oxford, the time after she had finally been forced to realise that Saul would never love her, that in fact he loved someone else. Oxford and Gareth Simmonds. Oxford, Italy—and Gareth Simmonds. *Italy* and Gareth Simmonds.

Picking up her coffee, Louise walked into her small sitting room and curled up on the sofa, closing her eyes. She didn't *want* to relive those memories, but she could feel the weight of them pressing down on her, pushing their way into her consciousness just as Gareth Simmonds seemed to be pushing his way into the new life she had made for herself.

As though the debacle of the masquerade ball had not been punishment enough for her to contend with, that following week she had received a letter from Gareth Simmonds. A curt letter informing her that he wished to see her as there were certain matters concerning her work which he wished to discuss with her.

Her parents knew she had received the letter, and

there had been no way she had been able to keep its contents a secret from them—although Katie had been sworn to secrecy over the worst of her excesses in skipping tutorials. If her mother and father had not actually stood over her while she went through the humiliation of telephoning Gareth Simmonds and making an appointment to see him, they had certainly left her in no doubt about their feelings of shock and disappointment at the way she had been abusing both her intelligence and the opportunity that going to Oxford had given her.

Furiously she had blamed Gareth Simmonds for adding to her problems, while having to give way to her parents' firm insistence that they would drive her to Oxford for the interview, where she planned to stay for a few days in order to try to catch up with her work.

They had set out after breakfast, her mother patently unhappy and trying to control her tears and her father unexpectedly grim-faced and distant, and Louise had known what was going through both their minds. Was *she*, like her elder brother Max, going to turn out to be one of those Crightons who had inherited the same genes as her uncle David—the 'S' gene, as she and Katie had nicknamed it as teenagers. The 'S' standing for selfish, stupid and self-destructive.

She had *wanted* to reassure them, to tell them that there was nothing for them to worry about, but she had still been deep in shock herself, still traumatised not just by *what* she had done but by the frightening emotions which had given rise to her dangerous behaviour.

'I can't believe you could behave so appallingly,' her father had told her grimly, his voice shaking slightly with emotion as he'd confronted her with the full enormity of what she had done after the ball.

'What were you going to *do*? Leave Tullah in the maze until—'

'No... No... I just...' Tears streaming down her face, Louise had turned her head away from him, not able to bring herself to admit that she had been so obsessed by her need to make Saul see her as a woman, to make him *love* her as a woman, that she had simply seen Tullah as a hindrance who was standing in her way. Someone who was preventing Saul from seeing her, Louise, properly, and recognising that they were meant to be together.

Katie had travelled to Oxford with them to give her some moral support. She was also going to use the time to see friends who'd stayed up in Oxford to earn some money waiting at the local bars and restaurant. While her mother had fussed around her rooms, tidying up Louise's discarded clothes and books, Katie had simply taken hold of her hand and gripped it tightly in a gesture of sisterly solidarity and love.

It was only when her mother had gone to shake her duvet and straighten up her untidy bed that Louise had finally moved, pushing her away and telling her fiercely, 'I can do that...'

What had already happened was shameful enough. To have her mother move her pillow and discover that she slept with Saul's purloined shirt beneath it would have been the ultimate humiliation.

When they were on their own Katie asked her awkwardly, 'Do you...do you want to talk about it...?'

Angrily Louise shook her head.

'Oh, Lou,' Katie whispered sombrely, her voice full

of pain and despair at what her twin had done, and love and pity for Louise herself.

'Stop fussing,' Louise commanded her.

'I'm sure Professor Simmonds knows what we've been doing,' Katie warned. 'I didn't want to say anything in front of the parents, but, as I told you, he's definitely rumbled the fact that I've been standing in at his lectures for you,' she went on. 'Have you got the notes I did for you?'

'Yes,' Louise acknowledged shortly. 'But how could he know of our switch? We've played tricks on our friends before now, and they've never realized.'

Katie waited several seconds before responding quietly, 'It's different with Professor Simmonds. He just seems to know. It's almost as though he's got some kind of sixth sense which allows him to tell the difference between us.'

'Some sixth sense?' Louise derided, scoffing. 'He's a professor of law, not a magician.' But even so she was left feeling uneasy and on edge. Something about Gareth Simmonds challenged her to defy him and to get the better of him, and it infuriated her that so far all her attempts to do so had ended up in her ignominious defeat.

'He called me Katherine,' Katie reminded her. 'Even though I was wearing your clothes and the others all believed I was you.'

'Arrogant, self-assured pig,' Louise muttered aggressively. 'I *loathe* him.'

But nowhere near so much as she loathed herself.

After Katie had left to let her sister draw her thoughts together—they had made the decision that, although they both wanted to go up to Oxford, they did not want to live together, nor to be thought of as an inseparable pair, and so were taking different courses and rented separate accommodation—Louise picked up the course notes her twin had left for her. But although her eyes skimmed over their contents her brain was simply not capable of taking in their meaning. How *could* it, when it, like her emotions, was still struggling to come to terms with the death blow that events had dealt her?

She had been in love with Saul and had dreamed of him returning her feelings for as long as she had been capable of knowing what being in love meant, and it had simply never occurred to her that she would not ultimately win him. Why should it? Every other goal she had ever set herself she had reached, and it had never entered her head that securing Saul's love would be any different.

Katie's writing started to blur in front of her eyes. Shakily she flung the papers down, wrapping her arms around her body. She felt so cold inside, so empty, and yet at the same time filled with such an enormous weight of fear and pain.

Automatically she went over to her bed and felt beneath the pillow for Saul's shirt, hugging it to her, closing her eyes and breathing in the warm Saul smell of him which still clung to it. But for once his faint but oh, so evocative scent failed to comfort her.

It wasn't his shirt she wanted to hold, she acknowledged as she threw it away from her with a wrenching shudder. It was the man himself. *Saul* himself. But he had made it cruelly plain to her that *that* was never going to happen.

'Saul, Saul, Saul...' Helplessly she cried out his name, whispering it over and over again inside her head as the tears started to flow.

Worn out by the intensity of her emotions, she finally fell asleep, only to wake up in the early hours, cold and shivering, her eyes sore and hot.

She was still fully dressed. She hadn't eaten, but she knew that the very thought of food was totally repugnant to her. As she got up she caught sight of the discarded notes that Katie had given her, and her heart gave a small, anxious thud.

Gareth Simmonds wasn't like old Professor Lewis. There was no way she would be able to sweet-talk him into overlooking the falling standard of her work—and Louise knew that it *had* been falling—but how could she be expected to concentrate on her studies when her thoughts, her heart, her whole self had been focused so totally on Saul?

'Ah, Louise. Good. Thank you for returning to Oxford at short notice. Did *your sister* come with you?'

Despite the calm and apparently friendly tone of his voice as he invited her into his study, Louise was not deceived by her tutor's apparent affability, nor by the way he'd emphasised the words 'your sister'.

Her plan of action, before her arrival here in Gareth Simmonds' study, had been to attempt to bluff things out, and to stick determinedly to the fiction that she had attended all his lectures and that *he* was at fault in mistaking her for Katie. But one look at his face, one brief clash between her own still sore and aching dark beautiful eyes and his far too clear and penetrative navy blue gaze, had been enough to alert her to the disastrous potential of such an unwise course of action.

'Sit down,' he instructed her when she failed to make any response—a first for Louise. She was not normally short of quick, sassy answers to even the most awkward questions.

It was a new experience for her to feel unnerved enough to hold her tongue and apprehensively await events. She could see a mixture of pity and irritation on his face that hurt her pride. How dared he pity her?

To her chagrin, she could feel her eyes starting to burn with the betraying sting of her emotions. Quickly she ducked her head. The last thing she wanted was for the urbane, controlled and hatefully superior man seated in front of her to guess that she wasn't feeling anywhere near as sure of herself as she was trying to pretend, and that in fact, far from not giving a damn about what he was saying to her—as she was desperately trying to show—she was feeling thoroughly and frighteningly vulnerable, and shocked by the situation she had got herself into.

Blinking furiously to banish her tears, she was unaware of the fact that Gareth Simmonds had got up from behind his desk until she suddenly realised that he was standing beside her, the muscled bulk of his body casting not just a heavy shadow but inexplicably causing the air around her suddenly to feel much warmer.

'Louise. The last thing I want to do is to make things hard for you. I know things haven't been…easy for you and that emotionally…If there's a problem that I…'

Immediately Louise stiffened. It had been bad enough having to cope with the mingled anger and pity of her family, but to have Gareth Simmonds offering her his lofty, condescending 'understanding' was more than she could bear.

'The only problem I have right now is you,' she told him aggressively, relieved to be able to stir up her own anger and use it to keep the humiliating threat of her tears at bay.

She thought she heard him catch a swiftly indrawn breath, and waited for his retaliation, but instead he simply said humorously, 'I know that legally you're an adult, Louise, but right now you remind me more of my six-year-old niece. I'm not your enemy, you know. I'm simply trying to help you.'

'Don't you dare patronise me. I am not your niece,' Louise retaliated, standing up, her cheeks flushed with temper, fully intending to storm out of his office.

But before she could do so he stopped her, taking hold of her wrist and gently but determinedly pushing her back down into her chair. And then, before she could voice her anger, to her consternation he knelt down beside her chair, so that their eyes were level as he told her, 'Stop making things so hard for yourself. You've got a first-class brain but it won't do you any good whatsoever unless you stop letting it be overruled by that stiff-necked pride of yours. We all go through times in our lives when we need other people's help, you know, Louise—'

'Well, I don't,' Louise interrupted him rudely, adding fiercely, 'And even if I did, the last person I would turn to for it would be you.'

There was a long pause before he finally said softly, 'That's a very interesting statement, Louise, and if I may say so, a rather dangerously challenging one.'

He was, Louise recognised with a sharp thrill of awareness, looking not into her eyes any more but at her mouth.

'He is just so sexy,' she remembered her fellow

female students saying when they talked about him, and now, like someone hurtling recklessly into unexpected danger, she knew exactly what they meant.

As immediate as that recognition, and twice as powerful, was her panicky, virginal rejection of it. She didn't want to see Gareth Simmonds as a sexually compelling and desirable man. She was only allowed to have that kind of reaction to Saul.

'I want to go,' she told him unsteadily. 'I…'

'Not yet. I haven't finished talking to you,' he had countered calmly. But he stepped back from her, as though somehow he had guessed just what she was feeling and wanted to make things just that little bit easier for her—which was totally impossible, of course. Louise knew that he disliked her every bit as much as she did him, and that he enjoyed making life difficult and unpleasant for her.

Holding her gaze, he said, 'Very well, Louise, if you want to do this the hard way then that's your choice. I do know what's been going on, Louise, so don't bother to waste my time or your own apparently failing brain power in trying to lie to me. In your shoes it would be pointless wasting the energy and intelligence you very obviously need for your studies on dreaming up unrealistic scenarios.

'In *my* experience there are generally two reasons why a student suddenly fails to live up to his or her forecast academic expectations. One of those is that quite simply, and unfortunately for them, they can't. By some fluke of fate and the examination board they've managed to get themselves onto a degree course they are in no way intellectually equipped to handle. The other…'

He paused and looked calmly at her. 'The other is

that for reasons of their own they have decided that they don't want to, that there are other and no doubt more important matters to claim their attention. The solution in both cases is, however, the same. For those who don't have the ability to continue with their course, to bring it to a swift end is, I think, the kindest way to end their misery. To those who have the ability, but who don't wish to use it... It isn't so much *their* misery one wants to bring to an end, but one's own, and that of their fellow students...'

Louise stared at him in furious disbelief.

'You're threatening to have me sent down. You *can't* do that,' she told him flatly.

Gareth Simmond's dark eyebrows had risen.

'No? I rather think you'll find that I can. But forgive me, Louise, I assumed that this must be what you wanted. After all...' he picked up her course work and threw it disdainfully across his desk towards her '...to judge from this, continuing with your course is the last thing you really want to do.

'Look,' he went on, when Louise continued to glare at him. 'If I've got it wrong, and the problem is that the work is too taxing for you, please tell me and I'll try my best to get you transferred onto a less... demanding course. There *are* university standards,' he reminded her, with deceptive gentleness, 'and I'm afraid that we do still strive for excellence rather than the mere pedestrian. If you feel that you're not up to the work—'

'Of course I'm up to it,' Louise snapped angrily at him, her eyes flashing. How dared he stand there and suggest that she wasn't up to the work? His predecessor had told her on more than one occasion, albeit perhaps in a roundabout way, that he considered her to be one of his most promising students. His predecessor... Louise clenched her fists.

'When a student's grades suddenly start to fall, *some* people believe that it's more the teaching that's at fault, rather than the pupil,' she challenged him feistily.

Gareth eyed her thoughtfully.

'Some people might,' he agreed coolly. 'But others might more intelligently suspect that the pupil's non-appearance at nearly half her lectures and tutorials might have something to do with the situation. Wouldn't you agree? I'm not a fool, Louise,' he said, at her look of surprise. 'I know very well that your sister has been standing in for you at my lectures.

'Look,' he continued, when Louise made no reply, 'we could argue about this all day. The fact is, Louise, that you've been skipping lectures and missing out on vital course work. And you've lost weight,' he told her abruptly, causing Louise to stare at him in astonishment. How on earth could he tell? Not even her twin or her mother had commented or appeared to notice—and with good reason, since she had taken to wearing loose baggy tops over her regulation jeans, knowing how much her mother would start to fuss if she thought for one moment that she wasn't eating properly.

Olivia's mother, although only a Crighton by marriage, had suffered from bulimia for many years, and her behaviour during the years of her marriage to David, her father's brother, had left its scars on the family. Her own mother was fervently keen on healthy, sensible eating—mealtimes, until Louise had left home, had been old-fashioned family affairs, with everyone seated around the same table. Not that

Louise had any problem with that—at least, not usually. She liked her food, and had a good healthy appetite, but just recently she had found herself unable to eat, too sick with longing and need, too hungry for Saul's love to satisfy her appetite with anything else.

'I appreciate that you're having personal problems…' Gareth said now.

But before he could finish, and suggest that she might benefit from talking them over with someone, she jumped in, demanding aggressively, 'Who told you that? They—'

'You did,' Gareth interrupted her levelly as he studied her mutinous face. 'You've lost weight. You're obviously not sleeping and you're certainly not working,' he reminded her quietly. 'The facts speak for themselves. I don't need a degree in psychology to interpret them.

'Professor Lewis told me that he confidently expected you to get a double first. On the basis of your current course work I'd say you'd be lucky to make a third. It's up to you, Louise. Either start giving your work some serious attention or…'

'You'll have me thrown out,' Louise guessed bitterly.

Without giving him the opportunity to say any more, she snatched up her papers and stormed angrily out of his room.

God, but she hated him. *Hated* him!

'Well, how did it go?' Katie demanded. She had been waiting anxiously for Louise to return from her interview and now, as she came hurtling out into the quadrangle, almost running, Katie had trouble keeping up with her.

'Slow down,' she begged her, catching hold of her arm, 'and tell me what he said.'

'He *said*... He *threatened* to have me sent down,' Louise told her flatly.

'What? Oh, Lou, no! Did you tell him, explain...? Did you...?'

'Tell him what?' Louise asked bitterly.

'About...about Saul... Did you explain? Did you—?'

Abruptly Louise stopped moving and turned round to face her twin.

'Are you *mad*?' she asked her grimly. 'Tell *Gareth Simmonds* about Saul?' She closed her eyes as she remembered the revolting pity she had seen in his eyes. How *dared* he pity her? How *dared* anyone?

'He's given me until Christmas to catch up...'

'Well, that shouldn't be too difficult.' Katie tried to comfort her. 'We've got the rest of the summer vac. And I can help you.'

'I don't *want* your help. I just want—' Louise began angrily, and then stopped.

The force, the futility of her own feelings frightened her. She felt oddly sick and light-headed.

'Why don't we spend the evening together?' she suggested to Katie, trying to make amends for her earlier bad temper. 'We could have supper and share a bottle of wine. I've still got that case in my room that Aunt Ruth gave us at the beginning of term. She said it would come in useful for student parties...'

'I'd love to but I'm afraid I can't,' Katie told her regretfully, shaking her head before explaining blushingly, 'I...I've got a date and...'

'A date? Who with?' Louise questioned her sister. But Katie shook her head and told her awkwardly,

'Oh, it's no one you know... Oh, Lou,' she pleaded as she turned to give her twin a fierce hug, 'I do understand how you must feel, but please, please try to forget about Saul.'

'I wish to God I could,' Louise told her chokily. 'But I'm not to get the chance, am I? Not if I get sent down and I have to go back to Haslewich. Oh, Katie...' It was on the tip of her tongue to plead with her twin to cancel her date and spend the evening with her, but then she remembered the look she had seen in Gareth Simmonds' eyes when he had told her that he knew she had been using Katie to stand in at his lectures for her, and she resisted the impulse.

She was not, she assured herself fiercely, the selfish, thoughtless, self-absorbed person his look had implied. She would have done the same thing for Katie...if Katie had asked...

But Katie would not have asked, a small inner voice told her.

The summer afternoon had given way to evening. Louise stared tiredly around her room. Papers and textbooks covered every surface, and her head was swimming with facts she couldn't assimilate; they floated in her brain like congealing fat on top of her mother's home-made stock, coagulating and clogging.

Saul. Where was he now...? What was he doing...? She got up and walked into her small kitchenette. She couldn't remember the last time she had eaten, but the mere thought of food made her feel sick.

Out of the corner of her eye she caught sight of Aunt Ruth's wine stacked in a dusty corner. Dizzily she went and removed a bottle.

Aunt Ruth had quaintly old-fashioned ideas about

how Oxford's modern-day undergraduates lived. The wine she had chosen for her great-nieces had been carefully selected for its full-bodied richness. Ruth had imagined it would be drunk at the kind of under-grad gathering that featured in expensive TV dramas—adaptations of books set in a glittering gilded era.

Louise opened one of the bottles and poured herself a glass. She was not normally a drinker. Oh, she enjoyed a decent glass of wine with good food, and she had gone through the normal student ritual of drinking at the bar in the students' union during the first few weeks at university, but that had simply been a rite of passage, something to be endured rather than enjoyed.

The red wine was rich and fruity, warming her throat and heating her cold, empty stomach.

Louise sank down onto the floor, owlishly studying the mass of paper she had spread all around her. Katie's handwriting danced dizzily before her eyes. Frowningly she blinked as she tried to focus and concentrate, quickly finishing off her glass of wine.

It was making her feel distinctly better—lighter, number. It was even making it possible for her to think about Saul without that wrenching, tearing pain deep inside her, threatening to destroy her.

Saul…

As she walked erratically back from the kitchenette, having refilled her glass, Louise tried to summon up Saul's beloved mental image and found, to her consternation, that she couldn't—that for some reason his beloved, adored features had become amorphous and vague, sliding away before she could crystallise them into a hard image. Even more infuriatingly, the harder she tried to visualise him, the more impossible it became. Instead, the male image that came most easily to her mind's eye was that of Gareth Simmonds.

Frantically Louise took a deep gulp of her wine, keeping a firm grip on it as she searched feverishly through her diary for the photograph of Saul which she always, always kept there.

Louise was clutching the photograph when she heard someone knocking on her door.

Katie... Her sister had changed her mind, cancelled her date realising just how much she needed someone to be with her. Tipsily, Louise lurched towards the door, yanking it open as she cried out, 'Oh, Katie, thank goodness you're here. I...'

Her voice faded away as her visitor stepped grimly over the threshold, firmly closing the door behind him.

'You!' she said shakily as she looked up into the merciless gaze with which her tutor had swept the room before finally coming to rest on her tear-stained face. 'What do you want...?'

'I came to bring you these,' Gareth Simmonds told her, and held some papers. 'You left them on my desk this morning...'

'Oh... I...' Awkwardly Louise reached out to take them from him, forgetting that she was still holding not just Saul's photograph but also a half-full glass of wine.

As she reached for the papers Saul's photograph slipped from her fingers. Immediately Louise tried to retrieve it, accidentally bumping into Gareth Simmonds as she did so, wine slopping from her glass onto both his wrist and her own arm.

Before she could stop him Gareth Simmonds was
bending down to pick up Saul's photograph.

'No. Don't...' she began, but it was too late.

As he picked it up he paused, studying Saul's features thoughtfully and then looking from the photograph to her face before declaring ironically, 'He's a
very good-looking man, Louise, I'll grant you that.
But is he really worth messing up the whole of your
future over? He's too old for you, anyway,' he added
dismissively.

Louise's temper, rubbed raw during her earlier
dressing down at his hands, burst into crazy pain.

'No, he's not...he's...' To her consternation she
felt fiery tears beginning to burn the backs of her eyes.
Pouring the rest of the contents of her glass down her
throat, she gulped rebelliously, 'I'm not a child, you
know. I'm a woman...'

The derisive look in his eyes demolished the last
of her precarious hold on her temper and pushed her
over the edge of caution into reckless fury.

'What is it?' she demanded. 'Don't you believe
me? Well, I am, and I'll prove it to you... Saul *would*
have wanted me if she—Tullah—hadn't come
along...'

'How much of that stuff have you had to drink?'
she heard him demanding as he ignored her furious
statement and removed from her hand the glass she
was still holding to sniff it with an irritated frown.

'Not enough,' she told him forlornly, adding aggressively. 'And give me back my glass. I *need* another drink...'

'No way. You've already had more than enough.'

'No, I haven't...' Angrily Louise reached out towards him, trying to snatch back her glass, but he was

holding onto it too tightly, and as he lifted his arm ᵤ remove it even further from her reach she lost her balance and staggered heavily into him. His body had all the unyielding hardness of solid rock, only it felt much warmer…warmer and…

Louise blinked as she realised that the heavy thud she could feel beneath her hand was the beat of his heart.

It felt oddly reassuring…*comforting*… Dizzily she started to frown as her alcohol-confused brain tried to assimilate this unacceptable information. She had the most peculiar desire to put her head against his chest, just where her hand was resting, and close her eyes, to let herself be comforted by that steady, sure heartbeat, like a child being soothed by the comfort of its parent.

Experimentally her fingers flexed and relaxed. She could feel the springiness of his body hair beneath the fabric of his shirt. Her eyes widened as she took in this additional information. Louise instinctively let her body start to relax against the warmth of his.

The arm he had raised to steady her when she had first fallen against him was still there, holding her, supporting her. She wriggled closer to his body and closed her eyes. She could smell the man-scent of him—so much stronger than the elusive, hard-to-reach scent that clung to Saul's shirt. This was the real thing, a *real* man. Louise breathed in deeply and appreciatively. His hand had moved to her hip, hard and warm through her clothes. She *liked* the feel of it there.

'Louise.'

The sharp warning note in his voice made her open her eyes and focus dizzily on him.

'No, don't go,' she whispered drunkenly. 'Don't go... I want you to stay with me... I want...'

He started to withdraw from her, and she read the stern message in his eyes. She quickly closed her own eyes and reached up with one hand to cup his face. She lifted her head and opened her mouth against his, using her other hand to take his hand from her hip to her breast.

As she felt the hard male warmth of his palm against her breast her body stiffened, quivering in excited expectation. The deep, tremulous breath she took lifted her breast against his hand. She felt his fingers curve into the shape of her body and his touch become a caress. The pad of his thumb stroked her nipple gently, and a quiver of sensual delight ran through her. This was what she had ached for, *yearned* for. Her tongue-tip stroked his lips, urgently demanding entrance, her breathing quickening in passionate arousal.

She had waited so long to be with him like this. Her teeth tugged pleadingly at his bottom lip as desire flooded through her. She could feel his lips starting to part as he gave in to her feminine aggression.

She had been *so* hungry for him to kiss her like this, she acknowledged dizzily as his mouth started to move over hers. She adjusted her body to get closer to him, and felt him shift his weight to accommodate her. A jolt of sensations rocketed through her, her inhibitions obliterated by the powerful force of the rich wine she had consumed. She felt as though she was floating on a high tide of incredible sensation. Her tongue darted wantonly into his mouth. She *wanted* him to touch her without her clothes, to feel his hands on her bare body. She *wanted* to touch him the same way—to absorb every last essence of him.

This was what she had been crying out for, starving for. *Dying for!* This, and *him*.

Against his mouth she cried his name...

'Saul. Saul... Saul...'

Abruptly Louise found herself being set free, *pushed* away from the intimacy of the male body her own craved so badly. Only his hands still held her, manacling her wrists as he shook her.

'Saul,' she protested.

'Open your eyes, Louise,' she heard a harsh and shockingly familiar male voice demanding bitingly. 'I am *not* your precious Saul, whoever he might be...'

Her tutor! She wasn't... This wasn't Saul at all. It was...

Abruptly she opened her eyes, gagging nauseously on the combination of too much wine, too little food and too much man—much too much man, her body told her as she reeled with shock. It was a lethal combination of strong wine mixed with strong emotion.

'I feel sick,' she wailed piteously.

'Oh, God,' she heard Gareth breathe irately, and then the next thing she knew was that he had picked her up and was half carrying her, half dragging her into her small bathroom, where he pushed her down in front of the lavatory—*and* only just in time, Louise realised as her stomach heaved and she started to retch.

It seemed like a lifetime before her stomach had disgorged its unwanted contents, but logically she knew it could only have been minutes.

Cold and shaking, she stood up, clinging onto the

edge of the basin, running the tap and reaching automatically for some mouthwash.

She still felt dizzy, confused, not really sure just what was happening. Clumsily she headed for the bathroom door, only to find herself being taken hold of very firmly and marched into the living room.

'Sit down and eat this,' she heard herself being told, and she was pushed unceremoniously into a chair and handed a plate of hot toast.

'I'm not hungry...' Apathetically she started to turn her head away.

'Eat it,' he ordered. 'My God, what's the *matter* with you? What the hell are you trying to do to yourself...?'

Louise felt her head starting to ache.

'Why don't you go away?' she demanded shakily.

'Not until you've eaten this,' she was told implacably.

Louise looked at the toast. Her stomach started to heave again.

'I don't want it,' she told him stubbornly. 'I just want—'

'Saul...' he interrupted her savagely. 'Yes. I *know.* You've already told me that...remember...?'

Louise blanched as she realised just what he meant. The alcoholic fog clouding her brain was beginning to clear with unwelcome speed. She looked at his mouth. Had she actually...? She could see a small swollen bruise marking his bottom lip, where she had... Quickly she looked away.

'I don't feel well. I...I want to go to bed...'

'Why? So that you can fantasise over your precious Saul?' he derided unkindly.

Louise closed her eyes. She could feel another

wave of dizziness surging over her. She tried to stand up and the dizziness increased. She could feel herself starting to black out. She tried to fight it, and then stopped. What was the point? What was the point in *anything* in a life that didn't have Saul in it.

Defeatedly she let herself slide down into the darkness.

When she woke up she was lying, still dressed, in bed, and Katie was sitting on a chair next to it, watching her. Her room had been tidied up and the air smelled fresh with polish and coffee. It was light outside, she recognised.

'What are *you* doing here?' she asked her sister groggily. Her throat felt sore and her head ached dreadfully.

'Professor Simmonds came looking for me. He said you weren't very well,' Katie told her carefully, avoiding looking directly at her.

Professor Simmonds. Louise closed her eyes, her body starting to shake as she remembered what she had done. With appalling clarity and total recall, behind her closed eyelids she could not only *see* the expression on Gareth Simmonds' face, she could even more demeaningly actually *feel* every sensation she had felt when she had…when *she* had…

Groaning, she rolled over, burying her face in her pillow.

'What is it? Aren't you feeling well? Do you want to be sick?' Katie asked anxiously.

'I… I… What did Professor Simmonds say to you about…about me?' she demanded frantically.

'Er…nothing… Well…he just said that you weren't well,' Katie told her, adding hurriedly,

'There's some kind of bug going round. Loads of people have gone down with it. He *did* say that if you wanted to go home immediately, without spending those few days sorting yourself out, starting the job of catching up...

'No. No, I can't.' Louise panicked. 'Saul...'

'Saul has taken Tullah down to see his parents,' Katie explained quietly.

'I don't want to go home,' she told her twin angrily, stopping to frown as she saw the way that Katie was avoiding meeting her eyes as she fidgeted with the pile of books she had just straightened.

'What is it? What have you done?' she demanded, with that intuition which was so strong between them, knowing immediately that there was something Katie was hiding from her, something she didn't want her to know.

Immediately Katie flushed.

'Tell me...' Louise ordered bossily. 'Tell me, Katie...'

'Uh...Professor Simmonds, when he came to look for me to tell me that you weren't very well, he said...he asked me about Saul...'

'He *what*? And *what* did you tell him?' Louise demanded, her eyes blazing furiously with temper and dread.

'I...I tried not to tell him, Lou,' Katie told her, begging her, 'Please try to understand... He was... I *thought*, from the way he was talking about Saul, that *you* must have told him—that *you* had said...'

'*What* did you tell him, Katie?' Louise demanded inexorably, ignoring her twin's attempts to sideline her.

'I told him what Saul meant to you... I told him... I told him that you love Saul, but that he...' Katie stopped and looked away from her.

'I'm sorry, Lou, but he was so insistent, and I...' She shook her head. 'He said you were ill, and I was just so worried about you that—'

'You told him about my emotions for Saul, matters personal to me. *You betrayed me*...' Louise cut her off in a flat, toneless voice that hurt Katie far, far more than if her sister had lost her temper and shouted and stormed at her.

'I thought he knew... He seemed to know. It was only afterwards that I realised...guessed... Lou, where are you *going*?' Katie demanded anxiously as Louise pushed her way past her and headed for her door.

But Louise didn't answer her. At least not directly, waiting until she had opened the door and was on the point of leaving before turning to Katie and telling her emotionlessly, 'When I come back, I don't want to find you here. Do you understand?'

It was the most serious falling-out they had had in all their lives.

Louise didn't turn back to look at her twin. She couldn't have seen her even if she had; her eyes were too blurred with tears.

How *could* Katie have betrayed her like that? How could she have told someone else something so personal about her? *Anyone* else, never mind Gareth Simmonds.

Gareth Simmonds. For a moment Louise was tempted to march round to her tutor's rooms and tell him just what she thought of him, but already the cool, fresh outdoor air was making her shiver, as her head spun with a weakening mixture of nauseating emotion and lack of food.

CHAPTER THREE

ABRUPTLY shaking her head to dispel her thoughts, Louise came back to the present. Her coffee had grown cold while she had been lost in her painful thoughts of the past and she would have to make a fresh cup. As she refilled the kettle and waited for it to boil she picked up one of the collection of smooth polished stones which decorated the open shelves, holding it cupped in her palm and smoothing her fingertips over its cool surface.

It had been a gift to her from her brother Joss. It was one of his most special stones, he had told her solemnly when he had given it to her, and holding it and stroking it would make her feel calm.

He had found it on one of his regular walks with Great-Aunt Ruth, with whom he shared an affinity for the countryside.

Louise smiled ruefully now as she closed her fingers around its comforting strength. It had galled her a little at the time, even though she had refused to acknowledge it, that someone as young as Joss had been so easily able to identify that part of her personality which she herself least liked.

The turbulence of her own nature offended her pride. She liked to think of herself as someone who was totally in control of herself, *and* her reactions. Perhaps because she needed to feel that they *were* under her control, because that was the only way she could reassure herself that the way she had behaved

under the influence of her intense adolescent crush on
Saul and the things she had done would never, ever
happen again.

Joss. Her smile deepened as she thought affectionately of her brother. He had all the virtues that Max,
the eldest of them, lacked. She had never met anyone
as well rounded, as complete within themselves, as
her younger brother. Even as a young child he had
exhibited an extraordinary degree not just of sensitiv-
ity and awareness of the emotions of those around
him, but also a compassion and a wisdom which
Louise had always secretly rather envied.

As she replaced the stone her eye was caught by
the small print that hung on the wall close to the
shelves. It was a sketch of the Tuscany countryside
which she had drawn herself while on holiday there
with her family. That had been the summer— Biting
her lip, she turned away abruptly.

After she and Katie had made up their quarrel over
what she, Louise, had seen as Katie's betrayal of her
in telling Gareth Simmonds about her crush on Saul,
that should have been the end of the matter—and of
Gareth Simmonds' involvement in her personal life.
But it hadn't been.

Briefly Louise closed her eyes. She had never been
back to Tuscany since that summer, although she had
spent time in other parts of Italy. Her parents thought
it was because she had outgrown the simple pleasures
of the family holidays they had spent there, in the
large rambling villa which they rented every summer
just outside the small, unpretentious little village
where they, as regular summer visitors, were on first-
name terms with all the inhabitants. But her refusal
to return had nothing to do with thinking herself too

sophisticated and grown-up for the company of her family.

Tuscany... Even now she could smell the warm, rich scent of the earth, feel the warmth of the sun.

By the time they had arrived at the villa that summer she and Katie had been talking again—*just*—and by a common but unspoken agreement nothing had been said or shown by either of them to their parents, nor the other members of the family holidaying together, to reveal that they had ever fallen out.

If, for the first time since their birth, apart from their choice of university courses, they were opting to do things separately, spend more time apart, then it had been put down to the fact that they were growing up and wanting to become individuals.

While Katie had stayed close to the villa, spending hours in the kitchen with Maria—the second cousin of the family who owned the villa, and who spent her widowhood looking after the villa's visitors—going with her to shop at the local markets and indulging her passion for cooking, Louise had set off in an ancient borrowed Fiat with her sketchpad to explore the neighbourhood.

It had perhaps been inevitable that the Fiat, unloved by the family who owned it and, perhaps more importantly, also unserviced by them, should have decided to stage a protest in the form of refusing to start one hot dusty afternoon, when Louise had returned to it having spent the morning sketching a small shrine she had seen at the roadside.

Recognising defeat when the Fiat had stubbornly refused to start after several attempts, Louise had looked up and down the empty road along which only one single, solitary car had passed that morning.

There was nothing else for it. She would have to walk to the red-roofed villa she could see set in the midst of an ancient grove of poplars lower down the hill.

The walk had taken her longer than she had anticipated, the road winding its way steadily downwards. The villa's wrought-iron gates had been closed, but she'd been able to see a car parked in the driveway. As she'd opened the gates she'd realised that the car had British plates which was a relief, although the thought of appealing to an Italian family for help hadn't particularly worried her. She was fluent in the language after so many holidays spent there.

She'd been perspiring stickily from her walk, and ruefully conscious of her dusty bare legs and sun-burned nose as she'd approached the villa.

When no one had answered her knock on the villa's front door she'd walked a little warily round the side of the house, and then stopped.

In front of her had been a sparkling, simple-shaped swimming pool, surrounded by an elegant paved area set out with sun loungers and decorated with huge tubs of cascading flowers.

Someone was using the pool, cutting through the water with an impressively fast crawl, brown arms neatly cleaving the water.

As she'd studied the seal-dark male head turned away from her an odd sensation had gathered in the pit of Louise's stomach, tiny quivers of unmistakable female appreciation running like quicksilver along her veins.

Irritated with herself, she'd turned away, her face suddenly warm with a heat that had *nothing* to do with the sun. The swimmer had obviously seen her, she'd recognised, because she could hear him heaving himself out of the water.

Warily she'd turned to face him, hoping her expression wouldn't betray what she had just been feeling.

'Louise! What...?'

Through the shock of recognising Gareth Simmonds' voice, two startling but totally unrelated facts hit Louise. The first was that he had instantly and immediately recognised who *she* was, even though he could quite easily have been confused as to which twin she might actually be. The second was that now, confronted with him, advancing towards her and sending droplets of pool water showering to the floor, and wearing a pair of black swimming shorts which she was breath-gulpingly sure ought only to have ever been on sale with a stern warning of the effect they might have on a vulnerable female, she knew that odd earlier frisson of awareness had *not* been a mere trick of her imagination. Dizzily she discovered that she was focusing on the exact point where the dark wet arrowing of body hair disappeared beneath the waistband of his shorts.

'My car's broken down. It won't start,' she told him breathlessly. 'I didn't...'

Quickly she fought to get control of herself, demanding aggressively, 'What are *you* doing *here*...?'

The look he gave her made her glower even more ferociously at him.

'What's wrong?' he asked her dryly. 'There isn't, so far as I know, any law that says holidaying professors aren't allowed to inhabit the same turf as their students. And I could, of course, ask you the same question. As it happens, my family own this villa.

They bought it about ten years ago, when they were holidaying here and fell in love with the area. Normally the whole family would be here, but unfortunately this year...'

'The *whole* family?' Louise questioned him, unable to stop herself.

'Mmm... I *do* have one, you know.'

'But they aren't here now...?'

'No,' he agreed.

'Have you got a large family?' Louise asked him, without knowing why she had done so. After all, why should she care?

'Mmm...sort of... I've got three sisters, all older than me and all married with children; they, along with my parents, normally descend on the villa for at least a month during the school holidays, but this year my eldest sister and her husband have taken their three children to New Zealand to see her husband's family.

My second sister and *her* husband and two boys are sailing with friends off the Greek Islands and my youngest sister and *her* husband, who, like my father, is a surgeon—there's a tradition of going into medicine in the family, and in fact I've rather broken with that tradition in electing to go into teaching rather than following my father and sisters into medicine—have gone with my parents to India. My mother is involved with UNICEF in a fund-raising capacity, and they've gone to see some of the work that's being done with the money they've raised.'

He spread out his hands in a dismissive gesture and told her dryly, 'So there you have it, a short, potted history of the Simmonds family. Oh, and I forgot, there's also my grandmother, who is very much in the tradition of a grand matriarch—though not exactly in the Italian style. My grandmother's forte lay in bringing up her three sons single-handedly after she was widowed, and in feeding their appetite for education rather than pasta—she's a Scot, so that's perhaps where *that* comes from.'

As he spoke he was reaching for a towel from one of the sun loungers, and briskly began to rub himself dry.

He had a surprisingly muscular-looking body for a university professor. Louise could have sworn that beneath his tutorial 'uniform' of soft Tattersall check shirt and well-worn cord trousers lay a body as misshapen as the old-fashioned knitted cardigans favoured by many of his older colleagues, but quite obviously she had been wrong.

He had stopped speaking briefly, and as she turned her head towards him she drew in a small, surprised gulp of air. He was rubbing his wet hair dry with the towel, his stance revealing the hard firmness of his belly and the strength of his upper arms.

Louise had no idea how long he'd been in Tuscany, but it had certainly been long enough to give his skin an undeniably warm golden tan.

'You're not feeling faint or anything, are you?'

His sharp frowning question made Louise's face burn, and she hurriedly averted her gaze from his body. What was the *matter* with her? She had grown up in the middle of a large, closely knit extended family unit, where the sight of the male body at every stage of its development, from babyhood right through adolescence, young manhood to middle age and beyond, had been so commonplace that until she had formed her crush on Saul she had been openly derisive of other girls' embarrassed and curious interest in the unclothed male form.

And yet here she was, breathing too shallowly and too fast, with a face that felt too hot and a potently explosive sensation low down in her body threatening her composure to the extent that she was having difficulty forming even the most basic coherent thought—and just because she had seen Gareth Simmonds wearing a pair of swimming shorts!

'Look, let's go inside, where it's cooler, and you can tell me exactly where your car is and I—'

'No. No, I'm all right,' Louise started to protest, but it was too late. He was already walking purposefully towards the open doorway to the house, leaving her with no alternative but to follow him inside.

If she had doubted that he might be telling the truth about his family, the number of photographs that crowded the flat surfaces of the heavy solid wooden furniture in the comfortably sized sitting room would soon have put her right. Even without studying them too closely Louise could immediately see the resemblance to him in the happy, affectionately close groups of people featured in the photographs. Her mother's small sitting room and her aunt Ruth's elegant small drawing room were similarly adorned with photographs of her own family, but that knowledge did nothing to alleviate the sense of anxious wariness that had gripped her ever since she had realised just whose territory she had unwittingly strayed into.

'The kitchen's this way,' Louise heard Gareth informing her as he led the way to the rear of the villa and the large, traditional farmhouse-style Tuscan kitchen.

'Sit down,' he instructed her firmly, pulling a chair

out from the table and then beginning to frown as she hesitated. To get to the chair she would have to move closer to him—*too* close to him, Louise recognised. He really had the most sexy and masculine-looking arms. The kind of arms you could just imagine locking tightly around you and holding you...the kind of arms...

'Louise.'

The sharp way he said her name penetrated the totally alien fog of shockingly unexpected feminine arousal that had momentarily swamped her.

What on *earth* was happening to her? It must be the heat or something, Louise decided hastily, still refusing to sit down as she repeated huskily that she was perfectly all right.

'If I could ring my father and explain to him about the car...' she told him.

'It might be easier if I took a look at the car first,' Gareth Simmonds argued, and Louise's face flamed, not with embarrassed confusion at her own inexplicable awareness of him this time, but with quick anger that he should dare to imply that she had not properly diagnosed the problem with the car herself.

'*You* won't be able to start it,' she warned him immediately, but she could see that he didn't intend to let her put him off.

'It's halfway up the hill,' she informed him. 'I'd stopped to sketch the shrine there...'

'Oh, yes, the Madonna. I know where you mean. Look, why don't you wait here, out of the heat, while I go and take a look?'

Dearly as she wanted to go with him, and see his expression when he discovered that she was right and the Fiat wasn't going to start, a small, inner, unexpectedly cautious voice warned Louise that she might be better advised to stay where she was. Even more unexpectedly, she actually found herself not just listening to it but actually agreeing with it as well.

She wasn't sure what malign fate had brought her here to be confronted by the person who, after Saul, she absolutely least wanted to see, but she *did* know that, given her extraordinary reaction to him just now, it would be extremely unwise of her to insist on doing *anything* that kept her in his company.

In fact, she knew that if she could just have summoned the strength to argue with him she would far rather have insisted on ringing her father and begging him to come over to fetch her just as soon as he possibly could.

Once Gareth had gone, having assured her that she was free to make herself as at home as she wished in his absence, she acknowledged that it was a good deal more comfortable inside the pleasant shade of the villa than outside in the full heat of the hot summer's day.

There was a bottle of Chianti on the table, and she was tempted to pour herself a glass, but, remembering what had happened the last time she and Gareth Simmonds and a bottle of wine had come together, she opted instead to pour herself a glass of water.

Taking it with her, she wandered back through the house, pausing to study the photographs in the sitting room. There was one there of Gareth Simmonds as a young boy, flanked by his parents, his grandmother and his older sisters. Hastily Louise looked away from it.

Outside, the water in the swimming pool glittered temptingly in the sunlight. If their own villa had one

drawback, it was that it didn't possess its own pool;
they had to share one with two other villas situated
close by.

Louise licked her suddenly dry lips. With any luck
Gareth Simmonds would be gone for quite some time.
He hadn't struck her as a man who could ever give
in easily to anything, and she judged that he would
be determined not to come back until he could prove
her wrong in asserting that the car wouldn't start.

Beneath the cotton fabric of her chino shorts and
her top, her skin itched with heat and dust. The swimming pool looked so very, very tempting.

Narrowing her eyes, she looked longingly at it and
then, recklessly dismissing the cautious voice that
warned her that what she was doing was dangerous—
when had that ever put her off anything?—she walked
very deliberately towards the pool and quickly
stripped off her shorts and top.

The weight she had lost in the months she had
ached for Saul had left her looking fragilely fine-
boned. Too thin, according to her mother, who had
been shocked when she had first seen Louise out of
her baggy shirts and in her more revealing shorts and
T-shirts. She was certainly too thin for Tuscan male
tastes, although she had noticed that that had not
stopped Giovanni, Maria's nephew, from making an
increasing number of excuses to come up to the villa
and flirt heavily with both herself and Katie.

Her skin, nowhere near as tanned or healthy-
looking as Gareth Simmonds', was just beginning to
lose its British pallor, but was more pale honey than
rich gold. Beneath her shorts she was wearing a pair
of plain white briefs, and under her top—nothing. Her
breasts, firm though they were, were still femininely

full, their shape disguised by the looseness of the top she had been wearing. A quick glance around the pool assured her that she had the place to herself. Gracefully Louise dropped into the water, deliciously cool against her hot skin.

Blissfully she floated lazily for a few seconds, and then started to swim. One length and then another, checking at each turn that she still had the place to herself. She was bound to hear Gareth Simmonds returning. The sound of a car engine would carry perfectly on the clear hot summer air.

She did another length, and then another, and then floated again for several seconds before some sixth sense abruptly made her roll over and flounder for a few seconds in the water as she opened her eyes.

Gareth was standing at the end of the pool, watching her. Cautiously she swam to the far side, where she had left her clothes and the towel which *he* had discarded earlier. How long had he been standing there? Not long—he *couldn't* have been.

As she pulled herself out of the water she could see him starting to walk towards her. Quickly she enveloped herself in the wet towel, shivering as it touched her damp skin.

'Take this one. It's dry.'

He was standing far too close to her, Louise acknowledged as she fumbled with the damp folds of the towel wrapped around her.

As she reached reluctantly to take the dry towel from him she could feel the one wrapped around her body starting to slide away. Quickly she made a grab for it, but it was too late. She could feel the heat flushing her face as Gareth's sharp eyed navy blue gaze thoughtfully studied her nearly naked body, but it wasn't her breasts his glance lingered the longest on, Louise noticed; it was her ribs and the narrow over-slenderness of her waist.

'You're still too thin,' he told her curtly, and before she could stop him, much to her chagrin, she felt him swiftly and practically envelop her in the dry, sun-warmed towel which he briskly fastened round her.

'I am *not* thin. I'm *slim*,' Louise retaliated through gritted teeth.

'You're *thin*,' Gareth countered grimly. '*And* you know it, otherwise you wouldn't be so defensive. I take it that your…that Saul isn't here on holiday with your family.'

Louise stared at him, her embarrassment over the fact that he had seen her virtually naked body forgotten as she marvelled not just at his memory but also his tutorial ability to make her remember that she was still his erring student.

'No, he isn't. *Not* that it's *any* business of yours,' she reminded him sharply.

'No? In so much as you are still one of my students—a student whose standard of work has dropped lamentably—it is *very* much my business. You were right about the Fiat. It won't start,' he added, before she could catch her breath to argue with him. 'I'll give you a lift home.'

'There's no need for that,' Louise protested. 'I can ring my father…and…'

'I'll give you a lift home,' Gareth reinforced as though she hadn't spoken. 'Give me five minutes to shower and get changed.'

'You might *think* you're a woman, Louise,' he told her astoundingly as he turned to go. 'But in fact, in many ways you're still very much a child—as you've just proved,' he told her as he glanced from the pool to her towel-wrapped body.

To Louise's chagrin, when Gareth drove up to the villa with her, her parents were standing outside, quite plainly having just returned home themselves. It naturally followed that she had to introduce Gareth to them, and explain not only what had happened to the Fiat but who he was.

'You're Louise's professor!' her mother exclaimed with a smile. 'Oh, poor you, coming all this way and then having your privacy invaded by one of your students.'

'I rather think that Louise believes if anyone is deserving of commiseration for the coincidence, then it's her,' Gareth advised her mother dryly.

Hospitably her mother offered Gareth a drink—but he hadn't had to accept, Louise fumed an hour later, as Gareth was still chatting, apparently quite happily, to her parents while *she* sat in silent resentment beside her mother. That was bad enough. But when her mother invited him to join them for dinner, and Gareth accepted, Louise wasn't sure which of them she disliked the most. However, a welcome diversion was fortuitously provided when Giovanni slouched round the corner of the villa, his face lighting up when he caught sight of Louise.

'Here comes your admirer,' she heard her father warning her. Louise tossed her head, suspecting that Giovanni was even more astonished than her father when, instead of irritably rejecting his unwanted and quite obviously sexually intentioned advances as she normally did, she not only responded to his soft-eyed looks and flowery compliments, but actively encouraged them.

'Oh, dear, Louise, was that wise?' her mother sighed once he had gone. 'Maria was telling us only this morning that his family are trying to encourage a match between Giovanni and his third cousin.'

'I wasn't actually thinking of *marrying* him, Mum,' Louise told her mother meaningfully, adding pointedly, just in case anyone listening—including her wretched and far too watchful tutor—had missed the point, 'He's got the most terrifically sexy body, though, don't you think?'

'Oh, Louise...' Jenny protested, but over her daughter's downbent head she gave her husband a rueful, slightly relieved look, which Louise caught out of the corner of her eye. She knew very well how concerned her family, especially her parents, had been about her crush on Saul, and they weren't to know that her pretence of being physically attracted to Giovanni had nothing to do with Saul but *everything* to do with the impassive and unwanted presence of the man seated next to her mother, silently watching the small piece of theatre being played out in front of him.

'I think I'll just go and see what Maria's planning for supper,' she told her mother airily, standing up to follow Giovanni who had disappeared in the direction of the kitchen and his aunt. 'Suddenly I'm rather... I'm...hungry...'

Tossing her head, she left her startled parents to exchange surprised looks as she stalked ferociously after her prey.

Once inside the kitchen, though, it was a different matter. Under Maria's stern eye, Giovanni's earlier swaggeringly macho display of flirtation quickly turned into bashful silence, and while Louise herself had been happy enough to encourage him while Gareth was looking on—how dared he imply that she was little more than a child?—now she lost no time in making it plain to the young Italian that she simply wasn't interested.

In the days that followed Louise very quickly came to regret not just encouraging Giovanni, who had now taken to following her around at every opportunity, but even more importantly running into Gareth.

An easy, relaxed friendship had very quickly developed between her parents and her tutor—even Joss and Jack seemed to enjoy his company, going off on long walks with him to explore the Italian countryside—and, whereas normally Louise would have been able to give vent to the pent-up irritation his almost constant presence in their family circle was causing her to Katie, there was a certain amount of distance between her and her twin still, a small and as yet not totally healed sore place from the quarrel they had had at Oxford—the quarrel of which Gareth himself had initially been the cause.

When her cousin Olivia, her husband and their little girl came to join her own family the situation, at least in Louise's eyes, became even worse.

Like Gareth, Olivia's husband Caspar was a university lecturer, and the two men very quickly hit it off, so that while technically Gareth was the one who was the outsider in their family group it was Louise who often felt on the outside of the comfortable closeness that everyone else was enjoying sharing.

Part of the reason for this was that she couldn't

quite bring herself to forget that Olivia was a close friend of Tullah's. Tullah, who had taken the place in Saul's heart and Saul's life that she, Louise, had so desperately wanted for herself. And, worse, Olivia had been there on that ill-fated evening when she, Louise, had behaved so stupidly and so...so dangerously, tricking Tullah into following her into the maze and leaving her there so that she could spend the evening with Saul. Only it hadn't worked out like that, and instead...

Watching Olivia and Caspar sitting with her father and Gareth in the sun one afternoon, Louise couldn't help wondering if Olivia had told *Gareth* about what she had done.

'Lou, why don't you come and join us?' Olivia called out cheerfully. 'I could do with some female support among all these men.'

For a moment Louise was tempted. She had always liked Olivia and, yes, even admired her—and, oddly, perhaps, for someone with her relatively competitive and ambitious nature, Louise had a very definite soft spot for small children, especially Olivia's little girl, Amelia. Louise had often gladly given up her own free time to occupy Amelia so that Olivia and Caspar could have some time alone. But today, seeing the way that Gareth broke off his conversation with Caspar to look at her, she fibbed quickly, 'I can't...I...I'm seeing Giovanni. He's taking me out for a drive...'

'Giovanni?' Olivia gave her an old-fashioned look, and Louise could see that she was surprised.

'Careful, Lou,' Caspar teased her. 'These young Italians can be hot stuff, and they aren't—'

'Will you all please stop telling me what to do and

trying to run my life for me?' Louise interrupted him angrily, her anger caused in reality far more by the fact that Gareth was an unwanted witness to Caspar's teasing than what Caspar had actually said.

'First you tell me to keep away from Saul, and now you're telling me to keep away from Giovanni. I *am* over eighteen, and who I choose to…to be with is *my* affair and no one else's,' she finished in a fierce voice, before turning on her heel and starting to walk away.

She was almost out of earshot when she heard Caspar saying, 'Phew…what did I do?'

'She still must be feeling very…sensitive about Saul,' she heard Olivia telling him. Bunching her hands into angry fists, Louise almost ran the rest of the distance to her bedroom.

No doubt by now Olivia and Caspar would be regaling Gareth with the full details of her wretched stupidity. Her cheeks burned, and to her chagrin she discovered that hot angry tears were splashing down her face.

Why, oh, why had she had to bump into Gareth like that? And why did he have to keep on coming round here? The rest of her family might have made him welcome, but surely he could see that she…

Since she didn't, in reality, have a date with Giovanni and since in reality dating him was the last thing she wanted, she was forced to spend the afternoon sulking in her room hoping that no one would realise that she was there.

CHAPTER FOUR

IT WAS during the last week of their stay in the villa that things finally came to a head.

Caspar and Olivia had already returned home. Katie, with whom Louise had still not totally made her peace, had gone out for the afternoon with the rest of the family, who had wanted to visit the local monastery, so that Louise was on her own. Even Maria was having a day off, which was no doubt why, she realised later, that Giovanni had decided to pay her an unexpected and unwanted visit.

She was lying on the sun-baked patio when he arrived, her bikini top untied and her eyes closed as she soaked up the hot sun and the even more welcome peaceful solitude.

The first intimation she had that Giovanni was there was when she heard his liquid voice asking if she would like him to put some suntan oil on her bare back.

Startled by his presence, she immediately turned over, and realised her mistake when she saw the way he was staring appreciatively at her naked breasts.

Immediately she reached for her bikini top, telling him at the same time that his aunt was not there and that he had better leave.

'I know she is not here, *cara*,' he told her crooningly. 'But that is why I am here. So that we can have some time together alone. I have wanted to be alone with you for a very long time, and I know that it is the same for you. Your eyes have told me so,' he teased her.

His own eyes were liquid with something that Louise judged had been ignited more by physical lust than tender emotion, but either way she was simply not interested.

'Giovanni…' she began warningly as she scrambled to stand up, but either he had misread the tone of her voice or he had decided to ignore it, because instead of giving her some distance he made a grab for her.

Thoroughly outraged, Louise tried to break free of his hold, but he was a strongly built young man, much taller than her and much, much heavier, and it suddenly struck her with a sharp thrill of fear that if he should choose to do so he could quite easily physically overpower her.

'Giovanni,' she began again, but this time, as she was all too uncomfortably aware, her voice sounded rather more hesitantly pleading than firmly assertive.

'Louise…what's going on?'

Never had she thought she would be so grateful to see Gareth Simmonds, Louise admitted as Giovanni immediately released her and started to say something to Gareth that she felt too shaky to catch.

Her hands, as she reached down for the skimpy top of her bikini, were trembling so much that it was impossible for her to fasten it, and instead she could only hold tight to it while wrapping her arms protectively across her naked breasts as Gareth told Giovanni curtly that he wanted him to leave.

'You *do* realise what could have happened, don't you?' he asked Louise sharply, once the noise of Giovanni's battered Vespa had died away.

Both his expression and his tone of voice immediately set Louise's back up. He was behaving as though he were her father, or her brother, as though he had a *right* to tell her what to do, to bully and correct her.

'Yes, I do,' she answered, her voice shaking as she added, completely untruthfully, 'And, for your information, I *wanted* Giovanni to make love to me...'

'To do what?' Gareth's voice dripped with cynical contempt. 'I doubt that *love* had very much to do with what he'd got in mind...' he told her derisively.

Louise's chin tilted dangerously.

'So he wanted to have sex with me. Is that so wrong?' she challenged him, tossing her head. 'After all, I've got to lose my virginity somehow, become the woman you're so keen to tell me I'm not. And since, as I'm sure you're now very well aware, thanks to my cousin and my loving, loyal sister, I can never share that experience with the one man...the *only* man I...'

Pausing, Louise bit down hard on her bottom lip. Why on earth had she got involved in this conversation, embroiled in this situation? Just thinking about Saul had made her heart ache, and filled her eyes with treacherous tears. Fiercely she fought to suppress them.

'It doesn't matter to me who the *hell* it is—who *he* is any longer.' Louise virtually spat at him. 'I just don't care...'

She had said more, far more than she had ever intended to say. Much more...too much, she acknowledged shakily. But instead of taunting her for her immaturity, instead of talking down to her as he had been doing all these last unbearably long weeks, she heard him saying in a voice that shook almost as much with anger as her own had done, 'Are you *crazy*? Have you *any* idea just what you're saying? Of course it damn well matters.'

'Not to me it doesn't,' Louise told him savagely. 'Why should it?'

Before he could stop her she turned on her heel and ran through the villa, up to the bedroom she shared with her twin.

From its windows it was possible to see the village, with its red-tiled roofs and the hillside beyond, but it wasn't the view that held Louise's attention, her eyes widening as she realised that Gareth had followed her upstairs and was now standing just inside her room.

'You dropped this,' he told her gruffly, handing her her discarded bikini top.

Automatically she reached out to take it from him, and then stopped as she saw the way he was looking at her.

'Keep away from Giovanni, Louise,' she heard him advising her grimly. 'He isn't...'

'He isn't what?' she demanded, anger flaring again. 'I don't *care* about what he isn't. I only care about what he *is*... He's a man, isn't he...a male? And he can... I'm tired of being told I'm still a child...not a woman. What does it take to make me a woman? As if I didn't know.

'I just want to have sex,' she told him defiantly, 'and I don't care who it's with...not if I can't have Saul...If I can't have Saul then it might as well be anybody...'

'You don't mean that,' she heard him contradicting her flatly. 'You don't know what you're saying...'

'Stop patronising me...' Louise was practically

howling at him now, so driven by the combination of her own feelings and his resented, unwanted presence that her reactions were no longer fully under her own control. 'I do mean it…'

'Oh, no, you don't,' Gareth was telling her sharply. 'And I'll prove it to you.'

Before she could even guess what he had in mind he had slammed her bedroom door closed and was standing between her and it—her and freedom. An ominous sense of things having gone too far began to trickle like icy water into her veins, but Louise wasn't going to give in to it and risk losing face in front of him.

'*I* lost *my* virginity to a friend of my youngest sister,' she heard him telling her coolly as he started to unfasten his shirt. 'She was twenty; I was just seventeen.'

Louise couldn't take her eyes off his body, his shirt…his hands… In appalled, paralysed fascination she watched as he finished unfastening it and shrugged it off. Calmly he started to reach for his belt.

Nervously Louise moistened her suddenly dry lips.

'What's wrong?' she heard Gareth taunting her. 'Having second thoughts…?'

'You…you can't mean this. You don't know what you're doing…' she whispered shakily.

'Yes, I can, and yes, I do. You said you wanted to lose your virginity. *You* said you didn't mind *who* you lost it to. I'm here, and I can promise you, Louise, that I'm perfectly willing and able to assist you. After all, it might as well be me as Giovanni, mightn't it…? *You* don't mind which of us it is, after all, do you? And forgive me, but it is quite some time since I've had sex, as the sight of your extremely attractive naked breasts has just rather forcefully reminded me.

'Men are *like* that, you know,' he continued conversationally. 'There's something about the sight of a pair of pretty, pert bare breasts that just naturally turns a man's thoughts to how those same breasts would feel filling his hands, how they might taste when he could get to suckle on them, how the *woman* they're a part of might react if he showed her...'

When he heard Louise's small shocked gasp he asked her quietly, 'What is it? I'm not embarrassing you, am I, Louise? After all, *you* were the one who said that it didn't matter *who* you had sex with, and, like I've just said, I'm more than willing to oblige you... *More* than willing... Here, feel,' he commanded, reaching out for her hand.

Louise stared at him in horrified fascination. What on earth did he think he was *doing...saying...*? He was her *tutor*. He was... She closed her eyes and then flicked them open again as, shockingly, she had a sudden explicitly clear mental image of him the way he had been that first day she had seen him climbing out of the pool at his own villa. Then she had been very much, if unwontedly, aware of the fact that he was not *just* her tutor but also very, very much a man, and now, suddenly and inexplicably, she was aware of it again.

'Did you...did you love her...your sister's friend?' she managed to ask him jerkily as she tried to drag her appalled gaze from his face. She did not *dare* to look at his body now that he had removed his shirt and was, it seemed, in the process of removing the rest of his clothes as well.

'I dare say I *believed* that I did,' he told her coolly.

'But at seventeen…I was *just* seventeen. What's wrong…? Louise, have you changed your mind…?'

Oddly, despite the fact that he had been talking to her for several minutes, he had still not unfastened his belt, and yet it had taken him no time at all to unfasten and remove his shirt.

Just for a second Louise was tempted to give in and admit that, yes, she had most certainly changed her mind, but her pride, always one of her own worst enemies, refused to let her. Give way, give in, and to him…? No… No… Never… And besides—besides, she knew perfectly well that he was only bluffing, and that he would never… Well, *she* could play that game just as well as him, and probably even better.

Her confidence returning, she gave a small toss of her head and told him firmly, 'No. I haven't.'

She pursed her lips and forced herself to make a thorough visual inventory of what she could see of him, determinedly lingering as long as she dared on the bare, bronzed expanse of his torso before quickly skimming over the rest of his, thankfully, still clothed body and returning her gaze to his face, saying, as disparagingly as she dared, 'You aren't as…as macho as Giovanni, but I suppose you'll still do.'

She saw at once that she had touched a raw nerve. A muscle twitched warningly in his jaw, but she willed herself to ignore it.

'By rights I ought to put you over my knee and…'

Widening her eyes, Louise willed herself not to blush as she asked him provocatively, 'Ooh, is that some special kind of position? I don't have your experience, of course, and—'

'You really are asking for it, Louise,' she heard him warning her, but she wasn't going to give in.

Shrugging, she told him tauntingly, 'Well, yes, I suppose I am... You needn't worry about me getting pregnant, by the way—I *am* on the pill...'

Her doctor had prescribed it several months earlier, when her emotional trauma had begun to have a disruptive effect on her normal monthly cycle.

'Very practical of you,' she heard Gareth commending her curtly. 'No doubt that was for Saul's benefit, was it? You do surprise me. I should have thought that deliberately encouraging, if not inciting the kind of "accident" that would have forced his hand and made him offer you and his child the protection of his name would have been more in keeping with the high drama of your infatuation with him.'

Louise's face blazed with angry colour.

'How *dare* you?' she breathed taking an impulsive step towards him. 'I would *never* try to trap a man like that,' she told him with fierce pride—and meant it.

'Louise,' she heard him saying almost wearily as he raised his hand and cupped the side of her face. To tell her what? Something she really didn't want to hear, she was pretty sure of that, and so far as she knew there was really only one sure-fire way to stop him.

Without stopping to consider the consequences of her actions, desperate only to silence him and have him stop dragging up the still raw pain of her loss of Saul, she quickly closed the distance between them, placing her mouth against his as she whispered, 'Save the lecture, Professor; *that* isn't what I want. What I want—'

She never got to finish her sentence, because suddenly and totally unexpectedly she heard Gareth groan

deep down in his throat, and the next minute she was
being dragged tightly against his body by his free
hand as his mouth opened over the prim closed shape
of hers and he proceeded to kiss her in a way she had
previously only experienced at second hand, via the
television screen.

She had known, of course, that people did, *must*
kiss like this—had even dreamed and fantasised about
Saul kissing her with just this kind of intimacy and
hard male heat—but the reality of having a man's
body pressed up hard against her own, the bare flesh
of his torso hard and firm and hot against the naked-
ness of her breasts while his hand cupped her face
and his mouth moved against hers with devastating
expertise and determination, was like comparing
watching someone else screaming through the air on
some wild fun-park ride with being the one sitting
there in the seat feeling that experience for oneself.

But no big-dipper ride, however terrifying, appalling and thrilling, could come anywhere near making
her feel what she was feeling right now, Louise acknowledged as she felt her whole body submit to an
avalanche of feeling—of sensation—of reaction—she
had *never*, ever guessed it *could* possibly feel.

She couldn't even control her body's urgent, hungry response to the skilled sensuality of his kiss, never
mind do anything about the way her breasts, her nipples were already aching so tormentedly for the kind
of caresses and intimacy he had described to her only
minutes earlier.

Briefly, bravely, Louise tried to fight what she was
feeling, to withstand the dizzying surge of hormone-
drenched arousal that swamped her, but it was a lost
cause, her brain no match for the clamouring hunger

of her body. Weakly she clung to the only solid thing she could find to cling to, her nails digging unwittingly into the hard muscles of Gareth's upper arms as she hung onto him for support.

'Louise.'

She heard Gareth protesting warningly against her mouth, as though he could feel what was happening to her and was urging her to resist it, but Louise *couldn't* resist it; she didn't *want* to resist it and she didn't want him to tell her to.

'No. No-o-o…' she moaned, pressing tiny pleading kisses against his lips, his jaw, his throat. 'No…Gareth… No, don't stop. Don't stop now…' she begged him, lost to everything. 'No, you can't. You can't…'

And to prove her point she pushed her body even closer to his, moving frantically against him, bestowing eager, feverish kisses against whichever bit of him she could reach.

'Louise. Louise… No. You…' She could hear him protesting, but at the same time his hand was reaching out to cup her breast.

Louise shuddered wildly in sensual delight as he touched her, urging him huskily, 'Do what you said you would do before… You said you wanted to taste me…them…' she reminded him, her voice sensually soft and slurred, her eyes bright with shocked passion, dilating in betrayal of her need as she focused blindly on him. And as she saw him hesitating she moved invitingly against him, arching her body against his, showing him the need she could feel pulsing so strongly through her veins and her senses.

The rest of the villa was empty, silent, the air in her room hot and languid from the afternoon sun.

Louise could see a tiny bead of sweat forming on Gareth's throat. She watched it in fascination as he tensed, his throat muscles rigid. Each second—each breath she took—seemed to stretch out for ever. Time itself felt as though it was standing still. She could see, hear, almost feel Gareth trying to swallow; the small bead of sweat moved. She reached out with her fingertip and caught it, holding his gaze with her own as she very deliberately transferred it to her tongue.

His whole body seemed to be caught up, galvanised by the fierce shudder that racked him. His hands cupped her breasts; his mouth covered hers. Louise shuddered in intense pleasure as wave after wave of sensual response flooded over her.

She could feel Gareth's hands, firm, broad, his fingers long and supple, shaping her as they slid down the silky hot flesh of her back before coming to rest on the rounded curves of her bottom. He bent his head, his hair brushing against her naked skin softly, in the most tenuous and spine-tingling kind of caress. She could feel the heat of his breath against her breast, and the delicate shivers of sensation down her spine became fierce, gut-wrenching, arousal-drenched waves of female need. He was caressing her breast with his mouth, gentle, slow, deliberately explorative kisses that drove her into a fury of impatience and longing.

Overwhelmed by her own need, she moved frantically against him. His mouth brushed her nipple, stiff and aching with the hunger that he himself had conjured up with his shockingly explicit verbal descriptions earlier.

She felt him hesitate, and her frustration boiled up,

bursting past what was left of her self-control and ability to think and reason logically.

Her hands found his shoulders, the flesh hot, and stroked the muscles and bone beneath, and their sensory message of his alienness, his total maleness, made her groan deep down in her throat—the same kind of feral yearning sound a hunting lioness aching for a mate might have made.

Her hands reached his back, strong and sleek, and urged him down towards her body. She felt the heat of his expelled breath against her nipple and shuddered uncontrollably beneath its impact. So might the hot peaks of a desert sand dune feel, when lashed by the scorching burn of the hot sirocco wind, the sensation both at once an unbearable aching pain and the promise of an even more intense and untenable pleasure.

'Do it... Do it...'

Not even hearing herself breathing the thick, urgent, guttural words had the power to shock or silence her, and the sensation that rolled through her as he gave in to her female command was not one of triumph or any kind of cerebral pleasure. Rather it was a form of relief so exquisite that she felt as though her whole body, her whole self was being drenched in a sensation so acutely intense that it was almost beyond her to bear it.

Rhythmically she moved herself against him, her hands going out to hold his hand as he drew her nipple deeper into his mouth, his earlier delicate, tentative suckling giving way to a fierceness, an urgency, that sent her delirious with reciprocal pleasure.

'Yes. Oh, yes... Yes...' she heard herself beginning to chant as her body writhed helplessly, no longer within her own mental control but totally and completely responsive to the male allure of his.

She was the one who reached for the fastening on his belt, and it was *she* too who urged and demanded that he remove the rest of his clothes.

'I want to see you, all of you,' she insisted to him. 'I want...' And then her voice and her body, her hands, grew still when she saw that he had given in to her pleas. Her whole body stiffened, a massive visible shudder running right through it as she gazed wide-eyed at him, slowly absorbing the visual reality of his body.

No need to question whether or not he wanted her; she could see perfectly well that he did. Tentatively she reached out and let her fingers slide down the soft arrowing of hair that neatly bisected his body. When she reached his stomach she could feel his muscles start to clench, but he didn't try to stop her.

The hair around the base of the shaft of his manhood was thick and soft. It clung to her fingers as though wanting to encourage her touch. Gravely Louise allowed herself to linger there a while, exploring the springy strength of the dark curls. Above her downbent head she heard him groan, and her naked breasts, her inner, secret womanhood throbbed urgently in a silent echo of the need he was expressing.

Her hand trembled slightly as she reached out to touch the hard, erect strength of him—her tremor wasn't caused by any feeling of trepidation or apprehension, it was simply her body's warning to her that it was as close to losing control as his low, raw groan told her that his was.

Delicately and slowly she explored the full length

of him, her lips parting on a soft, heavy breath of concentration.

Beneath her fingertips his flesh burned, his body rigid and hard. The sensual scent caused by the heat of their bodies filled the small, hot room, making her feel dizzy with longing.

Drawing back from him, she looked towards the bed and then at him, but before she could say anything he was removing her hand from his body and telling her thickly, 'You *know* me now, Louise, and now it's my turn to know you.'

Like someone trapped in a dream, without the power to move her limbs, Louise simply stood there while he removed her bikini bottoms. The sensation of his hands sliding down her thighs to remove them and then moving back up over them far more slowly and exploratively made her feel as though she was melting from the inside out. As she closed her eyes he stood up and picked her up in his arms, carrying her over to her bed. Laying her carefully on it, he started to touch her, caress her, licking her breasts. First one and then the other was given the moist attention of his tongue, and then his lips, suckling gently at first and then far more urgently on her nipples while she writhed and protested incoherently that what he was doing to her was too pleasurable for her to bear.

Slowly he kissed his way down the length of her body, his hands firmly parting her legs so that he could kneel between them, his fingertips stroking gently up the inside of her thighs. A soft, tormented moan escaped from Louise's throat, and her whole body started to tremble eagerly, helplessly snared in the unbreakable grip of her own arousal.

When his hands cupped her sex, and slowly and very deliberately started to explore it, laying it bare, not just to his touch but to his sight as well, Louise closed her eyes. Not because she felt self-conscious or inhibited, but simply because the sexual excitement exploding through her was almost too much for her to bear.

Within its intensity she could sense not just her own desire to push back the boundaries of her sexual knowledge and experience, but also her extraordinarily powerful female anger against herself, against Saul, against nature itself almost. Anger and love, love and anger—which of them was the stronger? Her body quivered feverishly beneath his touch, so delicate and yet at the same time so…compulsively needed, so…so addictive to her senses.

Inside her the desire tensed and coiled. Urgently she opened her eyes. He was bending his head towards her. She could feel herself hovering on the edge of a precipice, carried there, *hurled* there by the ferocity of her own need. Frantically she reached for his shoulders, whispering thickly, the words almost lost against his chest, 'Yes…oh, S… Now…now… I want you now.'

Her body was already quivering in the grip of its first pre-climax spasm of warning, and she whimpered beneath the force of it. He was moving onto her, *into* her, slowly—too slowly, her aroused senses recognised, and her flesh surrounded him with eager complicity, the jerky movement of her hips setting a fast and urgent rhythm that she could feel him trying to resist. Her hands slid down his back, urging him to thrust deeper within her. She felt him pause, resist almost, but her body wouldn't let him. Moist and urgent, more erotic and arousing, more *irresistible* by far than any practised sensual persuasion, it finally overcame and overwhelmed his attempt to hold back from her, and he began to move far more deeply and strongly within her.

It was like hearing her favourite, most emotion-arousing piece of music, looking out of her bedroom window at home on Christmas Day to see the countryside deep in an unexpected blanket of snow; eating her favourite food; having her emotions and her senses touched in every single way that aroused them, and all at the same time. It was all those things and more. All those things intensified a thousand—no, a hundred thousand times over, a sensation, a feeling, a *being* so, so intense, so perfect, almost beyond her capacity to bear its delight, that she thought when the fiercely strong climactic contractions surged through her body that the relief would cause her to break apart.

Afterwards, lying in Gareth's arms, crying and clinging to him as she fought for the words to tell him how magical, how mystifying, how awesomely unbelievably wonderful she had found the experience in between her emotional tears she could hear him telling her hoarsely that it was all right, that she was safe, that he was sorry. Somewhere between registering what he was saying and trying to respond to it she fell asleep, and when she woke up it was dark and Gareth was gone, leaving her tucked up in her bed, her bikini neatly folded on her chair beside her.

Downstairs in the villa she could hear her parents' voices, and then Katie came rushing into the room calling out urgently, 'Lou, wake up. We've got to pack. There's been some sort of emergency at home and we've got to go back. Dad's got us an early-morning flight...'

'An emergency... What...?' Louise demanded groggily, her thoughts automatically turning protectively to Saul.

'I don't know. None of us do. All I know is that Mum was on the phone to Maddy for simply ages.'

In the rush to pack up everything and make it to the airport to catch their flight, Louise simply didn't have the time to dwell on what had happened with Gareth, and anyway her lethargic, sensually sated body felt too complete and satisfied at that stage, too well pleasured and indolently disinclined to take issue with her mind about what had happened for her to do anything other than secretly luxuriate in the aura of sensuality that still clung to her senses, anaesthetising her against any need to analyse what had happened or why.

That came later, once they were back at home—hours of endless soul-searching and self-cross-examination while she went over and over what had happened, half inclined to give in to the temptation to comfort herself by believing that she had simply dreamed the whole thing. Dreaming about Gareth Simmonds in that way would have been bad enough, but of course she knew it was no dream.

The crisis which had brought them back to Haslewich, as Louise had guessed, involved her grandfather, who had developed a severe chest infection, and Maddy had rushed up from London to be with him.

'Mum is over with Gramps and Maddy. Maddy doesn't look very well herself, though Gramps is over the worst of it now. Joss was very worried about him.

You know what he's like?' Katie said, a few days after their return.

'Don't I just?' Louise agreed darkly.

Her brother had caught her off guard only the previous day by asking her if she had heard anything from Gareth Simmonds since their return.

'No. Why should I have heard anything?' she had demanded, red-faced. '*I* wasn't the one who kept on encouraging him to come round to the villa... *I* wasn't the one who went on long, boring walks with him.'

'They weren't boring,' Joss had contradicted her affably. 'He knows almost as much about the countryside as Aunt Ruth. He told me that when he was my age he used to spend his holidays in Scotland, with his grandmother. Anyway,' he had added, returning to her earlier question, 'he is *your* tutor.'

Was. Louise had been on the point of correcting him, but she'd stopped herself just in time. She had already made up her mind that she was going to change courses. The thought of going back to Oxford and having to face Gareth Simmonds now after what had happened made her break out in a cold sweat and shudder with self-loathing. How *could* she have behaved like that...?

While she and Katie were still talking the door opened and Joss came in.

'Could either of you drive me over to Gramps,' Joss asked winningly. 'I thought I'd go and see if there was anything I could do.'

'Why do you want to go over there?' Louise asked him curiously.

'I thought I could go and play chess with Gramps and give Maddy a bit of a break, so that she can go out and do some shopping or something to cheer herself up a bit…buy herself a new dress,' he added, with male vagueness.

'But Mum's over there with her,' Katie pointed out.

Joss shook his head. 'No, she isn't,' he told them. 'She had a meeting of the mother and baby home committee at three. She was just going to call and see Maddy on the way.'

'I'll drive you,' Louise told him, springing up and busying herself looking for a jacket, so that neither he nor Katie would see the emotional sheen of tears in her eyes brought there by the sudden awareness of just what kind of man her younger brother was going to turn out to be.

As she had promised herself she would do, Louise transferred to a different course and a new tutor once she was back at Oxford. Ironically her twin attended Gareth Simmonds' lectures herself now, but every time Katie mentioned him Louise very determinedly changed the subject and blanked her off, telling her quite sharply on one occasion, 'Katie, if you *don't* mind, can we *please* talk about something else, or *someone* else?'

'You don't like Professor Simmonds, I know—' Katie began.

Louise interrupted her, laughing harshly as she told her, 'It isn't simply that I don't like him, Katie—I *loathe*, detest and abhor the man, totally, completely and utterly. Do you understand? I loathe him. *Loathe* him…'

But she still dreamt of him at night that first term of the new year, and into the next—bewildering, confusing dreams involving a kaleidoscope of emotions and feelings from which she awoke in the early hours, her body shaking and drenched in perspiration and her eyes wet with tears.

The phone rang sharply, piercing her thoughts and bringing her back abruptly to the present. Quickly Louise went to pick up the receiver.

'Ah, so you are back. Why have you not returned my call?'

As she listened to the plaintive voice of Jean Claude, Louise reminded herself that she was no longer nineteen, and that she had come a long, long way from the girl who had cried out to Gareth Simmonds to make her a woman.

'When will you be free to have dinner with me?' she heard Jean Claude asking her.

'Not this week, I'm afraid,' she told him firmly.

'But *chérie*, I have missed you. It has been so long…'

Louise laughed.

'Stop trying to flatter me, Jean Claude,' she warned him, ignoring his mock-hurt protests. 'Look, I know very well that there are scores of women besides me in your life, so don't try to tell me that you've been spending your evenings alone and lonely at home…'

She could almost feel his ego expanding as she spoke. Despite his intelligence, Jean Claude was a particularly vain man, and Louise had already discovered that it was always easy to appeal to him through his vanity. That vulnerability in him, though, didn't mean that he couldn't be extremely shrewd and perceptive on occasion. He had already challenged her to disprove to him that the reason she had not, so far, gone to bed with him was because emotionally there was another man in her heart, if not in her life. But she wasn't going to resurrect *that* particular argument right now.

'My boss has a big meeting in the morning, which could drag on, and then there's a formal dinner at night…'

'The committee which is to look into the fishing rights of the Arctic seas—yes, I know,' Jean Claude acknowledged. 'Our governments will be on opposite sides on this matter, I suspect.'

Louise laughed.

'Perhaps we shouldn't see one another for a while, then,' she teased him. 'Just in case!'

To her surprise, instead of sharing her laughter, Jean Claude's voice became unusually grave as he told her, 'This is an extremely serious matter for us, *chérie*. Our fishermen need to be able to fish in those waters. Yours…'

Louise could almost see him giving that small Gallic shrug he so frequently made.

'Yours have an area of sea—of seas—to fish which far exceeds the land mass which is your country…'

'A legacy from the days when Britannia ruled the waves,' Louise joked ruefully, but Jean Claude continued to remain serious.

'Such colonialist views are not considered acceptable in these modern times *petite*', he reminded her. 'And if you would accept a word of warning from me I would suggest that you do not voice them too publicly. There are many nations based here in Brussels who consider that they have good reason to resent what they view as British tyranny and oppression…'

It was on the tip of Louise's tongue to point out mildly that the French, along with the Dutch, and the Portuguese, come to that, had all been equally vigorous at some stage of their history in pursuing the acquisition of new colonies, lands and seas over which they staked ownership, but Jean Claude's serious tone prevented her, and besides, as she had often noticed, sensationally handsome and attentive though he was, for her tastes the Frenchman lacked one vitally important virtue: he had virtually no sense of humour.

'It's going to be next week before I can see you, Jean Claude,' she told him instead.

'Very well...then I shall ring you next week. Although we could always be together later...after your dinner is over...' He started to purr meaningfully.

Louise laughed.

'Spend the night with you, you mean... *Non. Non, non...*'

'Now you say *non*, but one day soon you will say *oui*, and not just to spend the night with me,' he warned her, and she could hear the smile of satisfaction in his voice as she laughed and said her goodbyes.

'You're wrong, Jean Claude,' she murmured to herself as she replaced the receiver. Attractive though he was, she was in no danger of being tempted to join his long list of lovers.

'Oh, but you are so cold,' he had complained the last time she had refused him. 'Cold outside, but I think *very*, very hot inside. Very, very hot...' he had whispered as he had attempted to deepen the passion of the kiss they were sharing.

'Why so bashful?' he had added when she had gently, but firmly, disengaged herself from him. 'You are a woman of very great attractiveness, Louise, and

I cannot be the first to tell you so—nor the first man to take you to bed...'

'*You* haven't taken me to bed,' Louise had felt bound to remind him.

'Not yet,' he had agreed, adding wickedly, 'But I shall...and very soon.' His voice had deepened as his hand reached out to stroke her breast.

Deftly Louise had manoeuvred herself away from him and opened the door of his car.

He was right about one thing. He was not the first to have wanted to take her to bed, but...

'Oh, no... *No*,' Louise told herself fiercely. 'I'm not going through all that again. I'm not travelling down that road...thinking *those* thoughts...'

Wasn't it one of the first signs of long-term spinsterdom when one started talking to oneself...?

Spinsterdom... It was an old-fashioned, very non-politically correct and out-of-favour word, with all its unkind connotations and in-built prejudices. But a spinster was, after all, what she was, and what she was likely to remain...

By choice, she reminded herself fiercely. By *choice*. By the expression of her *free will* because... because...

'Stop that,' she told herself sternly, reminding herself mundanely, 'You've got to be up early in the morning!'

CHAPTER FIVE

'LOUISE. Good!' her boss greeted her as she hurried into Louise's office. 'I'm glad you're here early.'

'I thought you'd want me to brief you on the possible legal complexities of this proposed change in fishing rights.'

'Yes, yes, I do,' Pam Carlisle agreed. 'But I also want you to accompany me to this morning's meeting. Things have changed rather a lot since we first discussed the matter. For a start, there's been a good deal of political argument brought up by some of the other committee members over the fact that the proposed Chair, Gareth Simmonds, is British, and of course the existing fishing rights are also British.'

'Yes... Yes, so I understand,' Louise agreed tensely, keeping her face averted from her boss as she fiddled with some papers on her desk.

'You know? But how?'

'My sister told me, and as it happens Gareth Simmonds was on the same flight as me. I... He was my tutor for a while when I was up at Oxford,' Louise explained brusquely. There—it was said...out...over and done with.

'Oh, you know Gareth, then.' Pam beamed at her. 'We're most frightfully lucky to have had him agree to accept the Chair, and, as I've already pointed out to the other committee members, they simply couldn't have a chairperson who could be less biased. Well, if he was your tutor *you* must know that. He really is the most— It's just as well I'm a very happily married woman,' she told Louise frankly, with a wide grin. 'I can tell you, Louise, when he smiled at me I could practically feel myself melting. His students must have fallen for him like ninepins, poor man...'

'Poor man? *Why* poor man?' Louise asked, rather more sharply than she had intended, she could see, as Pam gave her a puzzled look.

'Oh, dear, Lou, have I trodden on an Achilles' heel?' She asked, with amusement. 'Did you have a bit of a thing for him while you were an undergrad?'

'No. I most certainly did not,' Louise denied vehemently, her colour suddenly very high and her eyes spitting sparks of anger. 'If you want the truth...' She paused, only too well aware of the danger she was running into.

'Yes...?' Pam prompted.

'Oh, nothing,' Louise hedged. 'Look, I've produced a list of possible points that may be raised, and, of course, there's always the chance that we're going to have that old accusation of colonialism thrown at us...'

'Colonialism...?' Pam raised her eyebrows. 'Well, I suppose you *could* be right, and it's certainly best to be prepared for everything.'

Louise, who knew the situation equally as well as her boss, nodded. 'It's going to be my job to persuade the committee that we need to keep fishing quotas down and retain as much control over our fishing rights as we can. It's not going to be easy...'

'No,' Louise agreed. 'I've read up as much as I can on maritime law, and, of course, all the other legal facts that cover the situation. I've prepared several briefs for you on the subject, and I'm also getting hold of translations of the law and legal histories that the other committee countries are likely to be using as counter-arguments.'

'Mmm…looks like I'm going to be doing an awful lot of reading.'

'Well, I'll condense as much of it as I can, and, of course, if a point is raised that needs further exploration…'

'You'll deal with it. Yes, I know you will, Lou. Have I told you recently, by the way, what a treasure you are? When Hugh first recommended you to me I admit I *was* rather dubious…but he convinced me that you would be up to the job and he was more than right.'

Hugh Crighton was Saul's father, her grandfather's half-brother. Initially a barrister, and now a semi-retired judge, he lived in Pembrokeshire with his wife Ann, and it was from living in a coastal area that he had become acquainted with the European MP Pam Carlisle, for whom Louise now worked.

Originally, when she had been offered the job, Louise had resentfully assumed that this was her uncle Hugh's way of getting her out of his son's life. But at a family gathering Hugh had taken her on one side and told her gently, 'I know what you're thinking, Lou, but you're wrong. Yes, I *do* think it's a good idea for you and Saul to have some distance between you, and for Tullah and Saul to be allowed to build their new life together, but I also happen to think that you're ideally suited for this kind of work. You've got the right kind of fighting spirit it needs.'

'I wanted to be a barrister,' Louise had reminded him.

'Yes, I know,' he had acknowledged. 'But, my dear Lou, you're too hot-blooded and—'

'Too hot-tempered,' she had supplied angrily for him.

'Spirited,' he had amended. 'A crusader...a leader. You need the kind of challenge this work specifically will provide.'

And, of course, he had been right, and if she was honest, the thought of practising law in the dry, dusty courts of the European legal system did not appeal to her any more.

'You just want to be a barrister so that you can prove to Gramps that you're better than Max,' Joss had commented calmly at that same gathering. 'But it's all right, Lou,' he had told her in a kind voice. '*We* all know that you *are* better...'

Better... What did that mean? she wondered now. What had happened to the young woman who had declared that if she couldn't have Saul then all she wanted in compensation was to be materially successful, to make her mark in the world? Why was she suddenly beginning to feel that there might be something missing from her life, that there might be *someone* missing from it?

'Lou? Are you all right...?'

'Yes. Yes, I'm fine,' she assured Pam Carlisle, swiftly gathering up the papers she would need as she prepared to follow her out to the waiting car.

En route to their destination, Louise studied their surroundings absently through the car window. Brussels, despite hearsay to the contrary, was, in fact, a beautiful city; but it was true it *was* a majestic and very proper kind of rigid beauty that perhaps could not always be easily appreciated. But beautiful it was, nevertheless, Louise acknowledged as the driver brought the car to a halt and got out to open the doors for them.

Several of the other committee members and their assistants had already arrived. Louise knew most of them by sight if nothing else. Brussels' political circles were surprisingly small, in view of the number of politicians and ancillary workers and diplomats who worked at the commission.

She was grimly amused to see that the French representative had with him a particularly aggressive and highly qualified legal adviser big-wig, who Louise suspected was far more used to running his *own* committees rather than sitting in a back seat capacity on someone else's. She had never actually met him before, but knew of him by reputation, and, as she whispered discreetly to her boss, it proved how seriously the French were taking the issues that they should have supplied their representative with someone so very senior.

'This is a very serious political issue for them,' Pam Carlisle agreed. 'Even more so in many ways than it is for us. But it's the Spanish contingent we should expect to have the most trouble with.

'Oh, look, there's Gareth Simmonds just walking in,' Pam told her, but Louise had already seen him.

His dark, impeccably tailored suit emphasised the masculine power of his shoulders—and their breadth. Beneath the pristine crispness of his shirt Louise could see his chest rising and falling as he breathed. Was it still bisected by that same dark arrowing of soft, finger-magnetising dark hair? Did he still...?

Angrily, she turned her head away.

'I'd like to have a word with him, but I've been

warned to be especially careful. We can't afford to take any risks of having him accused of favouritism,' Pam commented.

'Strictly speaking he shouldn't be in a position to favour *anyone*,' Louise reminded her dryly. 'The issue is to be resolved by sticking to the *law*.'

From the past Louise could almost hear Gareth Simmonds' voice as he lectured them on the finer points of European law, his tone becoming increasingly passionate as he pointed out to them that the way ahead lay not so much in the British law courts, but in those of the new European parliament.

'New community laws will be written which will supersede the old, nationalistic laws, and the responsibility for making those laws could well lie in your hands...'

The meeting was being called to order. Out of the corner of her eye Louise watched Gareth. He was deep in conversation with a stunning blonde whom Louise recognised as one of the phalanx of legal advisers attached to the German embassy—Ilse Weil. From her body language, it was quite plain that it wasn't just Gareth's attention as the chairperson of the committee she was courting, Louise decided derisively. And, what was more, Gareth Simmonds didn't seem to be doing anything to put a less intimate distance between them.

Abruptly, she turned away. If Gareth Simmonds chose to respond to another woman's sensual come-on, then that was no business of *hers*. No business at all. Nor was there any way she would ever want it to be.

'Thanks, Lou... I appreciate the way you handled everything. We were faced with some pretty tricky questions, and I could be wrong, but I've got a gut feeling that one or two people were quite definitely caught off guard by the answers you were able to come up with.'

'Mmm... I wouldn't be *too* optimistic,' Louise warned her boss, adding dryly, 'We *are*, after all, dabbling in pretty murky waters...'

'Murky, maybe, but hopefully legally within our territory,' Pam responded with a grin. 'You haven't forgotten we've got this wretched dinner tonight as well, have you?'

Louise shook her head.

'I must say that I'm not particularly looking forward to it—all that boring small talk. *Why* is it that diplomatic small talk is even worse than any other kind?'

Louise laughed. 'Cheer up,' she consoled her boss. 'Only another few days and then you'll be going home.'

Her boss had some leave she was due, which she had decided to take to coincide with her husband's early retirement from the local government department he headed.

'Once Gerald has retired, at least we'll be able to spend a bit more time together. Although I'm not sure how well he's going to adapt to living here in Brussels,' she confessed.

Louise suspected that it wasn't so much Brussels her boss was concerned about her husband adapting to as the fact that he would be living there rather in her shadow.

The nature of her job meant that Louise rarely worked normal office hours, and so she had no qualms about her plan to head straight back to her apartment now the meeting was over. She had some reading up she wanted to do, and one or two other things. A couple of points had been raised at the meeting that she wanted to check up on, and then, she decided luxuriously, she would probably go for a swim. The apartment block where she lived had its own gym and in-house swimming pool facilities, which Louise used as regularly as she was able.

Ilse Weil had collared Gareth Simmonds again, she noticed as she started to collect her papers together. Much as it went against the grain for her to have to admit it, he *had* chaired the meeting extremely well. She had almost been able to see the committee members' respect for him growing as he'd dealt courteously but firmly with some of their more outrageous claims and counter-claims.

From a legal point of view, of course, his grasp of the subject would be absolutely first class.

Out of the corner of his eye Gareth watched Louise turn to leave.

He had known, of course, that she was working in Brussels, and it had been perhaps inevitable that they should run into one another. It hadn't been altogether welcome news for him to discover that the British representative on the committee had Louise working for her as her assistant, but by then it had been too late for him to back out.

Seeing her on the plane had been a shock that he hadn't been expecting, and he could still feel the after-effects of the jolt that had hit him like a surge of electricity when he had stood up and seen her.

Ilse Weil was still talking to him. He bent his head towards her and smiled politely. She had long blonde hair and good skin. Beneath the fine wool of her top he could see the firm jut of her breasts, her nipples discreetly outlined. Male instinct told him that she would be far from cool in bed, but his body refused to be impressed—or aroused.

Louise… She had had her hair cut short, a gamine crop. It suited her, revealing the perfection of her delicate bone structure, making her look somehow more feminine and fragile than she had done with it long. Her clothes, unlike Ilse's, did not reveal the curves of her breasts, and there was certainly no suggestion of any tempting thrust of an aroused nipple beneath the shirt she was wearing under her suit jacket. He had seen the flash of dislike in her eyes when she had seen him earlier, just as he had seen it on the plane. She had quite obviously still not forgiven him for what had happened that summer in Tuscany.

'Gareth?'

'I'm sorry, Ilse. I missed what you were saying.' He was forced to apologise as she placed a smooth white hand on his arm. Her nails were painted an immaculate glossy dark red. They were long and elegantly manicured. Louise's nails were short and unpolished, or at least they had been that summer in Tuscany. But they had still been long enough to leave long, raised, passion-driven weals in his skin, on his arms and his back where she had raked him with them in the frantic intensity of her sexual passion—but not for him. *Her* passion had not been for him. His mouth hardened. Had it been deliberate, the way she had tangled his name with another man's as she'd pleaded with him to satisfy her, to take her, to…?

'I'm sorry, Ilse. I really must go.' He interrupted his companion.

Immediately she pouted, her finger curling round the cloth of his sleeve.

'Oh, but I hadn't finished... But then I shall see you tonight at the dinner.' She gave him a flirtatious look. 'Perhaps I might even arrange for you to sit next to me...'

'I rather think the other members of the committee will have something to say if they think I'm paying you too much attention,' Gareth told her gently, before retrieving his arm.

An affair with a woman who threatened to be as tenacious as Ilse was obviously the last thing he wanted. An affair with *anyone* was the last thing he wanted... He closed his eyes for a moment and leaned against the wall. What he *wanted*...what he wanted was, ironically, what his mother and his married sisters were continually telling him he *needed*. A wife, children...a family... Louise!

All of those things, those life fulfilments, were denied to him, though, and had been denied to him since that fateful summer's day in an Italian villa when he had wilfully, stupidly, and for ever and ever, heartachingly, life-challengingly allowed his emotions to overrule his intelligence.

Now, for him, there could be no happy-ever-afters. How could there be when he knew, had known, from the moment he touched her, that any other woman than Louise could only and for always be second best? And that any children he might have with her, no matter how much loved, would always stand in the shadow of the children he might have had with Louise.

He had known, of course, all along, that she had not shared the explosive, mind-shattering moment of stark truth and self-knowledge he had been forced to endure, that for her there had been no savage, searing pain of recognition for the emotional significance of what was happening, no realisation that here was something that wasn't going to remain hidden by the anger he was using to mask it, and that he was deluding himself by trying to convince himself that his reaction to her was merely physical.

He had been under no illusions; she had simply been punishing herself, trying to destroy her love for another man in the fierce heat of what they had shared. She had not emerged from the inferno of their lovemaking with her emotions transformed, transmuted, from the base metal of lust into the pure gold of love—but he had. Oh, yes, he most certainly had.

He had tried to contact her the following day, telling himself that it was the right thing to do, the responsibly aware thing to do, but when he had initially telephoned and then called round at the villa he had found it empty. It had been another day before he had been able to make contact with Maria and discover that an emergency had taken the family home.

On his own return to Britain he had tried again— telephoning Louise's home in Cheshire. Jenny had answered the telephone, her voice warm with recognition as he'd explained that he had learned from Maria that they had had to leave before the end of their holiday.

She had thanked him for telephoning and had written down his number when he had proffered it—'just in case Louise wanted to have a chat with me before the new term starts'.

There had been a brief but very significant pause before Jenny had told him a little uncomfortably that Louise had told her parents she had decided to change courses.

He had known then, of course, that what had happened between them was something that Louise didn't want to pursue. And he had told himself firmly that he was a mature, thinking man and that he would somehow get over what he was feeling.

And in a way he had. He no longer woke up every morning longing for her, and the memory of the time they had spent together was something he only allowed himself to relive very, very occasionally—or at least it had been.

His family thought the reason he hadn't married was that he was too choosy...too dedicated to his work.

'If you're not careful, you're going to end up a lonely old man,' they had warned him as, last Christmas, they'd plucked a miscellany of small children and large animals from his prone body.

'If you're not careful I shall be a *grandmother* before you're a father,' his eldest sister had told him direfully.

Since her eldest child, a girl, had not yet reached her teens, Gareth had felt impelled to deny this statement, but the truth was that, much as he would like to be married, to have for himself the obvious happiness and contentment that existed for his sisters with their partners and their families, there was one vital component missing from his life that made this scenario impossible.

He needed to find *someone* he could *love*—someone who would love him in return. He was a long way past the age when the excitement of mere sexual lust, no matter how strong, was enough to convince him that it was a sound basis for a long-term relationship.

'Please don't blame Lou for…for… She can't help it,' her twin sister Katie had told him, her voice trembling slightly as though she could feel an echo of her sister's pain. 'It's because she's in love.'

In love… Oh, yes, Louise had been in love…!

'If I can't have Saul then it might as well be anybody…' she had told him passionately, when he had pointed out to her the consequences of her flirtation with the young Italian nephew of the villa's housekeeper.

Anybody… Even *him*… Wearily Gareth bowed his head. There was pain and then there was guilt, and of the two of them…which did he find it hardest to bear? The knowledge that he couldn't control his emotions, or the knowledge that he couldn't control himself? Both were spirit-crushing, heart-numbing emotions, but of the two… He looked again at Louise, and for some reason she stopped what she was doing and looked back at him. Even at this distance he could see the rejection and the dislike in her eyes. What would she say, he wondered, if he were to go over to her and tell her…take her…?

Having watched Gareth lever his shoulders away from the wall on which he had been leaning, Louise looked abruptly away from him. When she picked up the last pages of her notes she saw that her hand was trembling. Stuffing the pieces of paper into her case, she warned herself that she couldn't afford to give way to her emotions.

She hated the knowledge that he had about her, the fact that she could *never* take back the power she had given him over her, the fact that she could *never*, ever forget or wipe out what had happened between them. Even now there were times when she came awake from her dreams with his name on her lips, when she could hear an echo, the sound of her own voice calling out to him in the throes of her agony of sexual need. She had been a virgin, and yet, in the space of those few hours, her body had flowered, burst into full womanhood in a way that had left her feeling as though she hardly knew herself at all.

All her dreams of sex with Saul had centred on the thrill of finally having him to herself, of *his* desire for *her*, *his* arousal, *his* need. Naively she'd visualised him begging her to allow him to touch her body. It had simply never occurred to her that *she* might be the one doing the begging, that *her* emotions, *her* desires might be the ones that were out of control, that *she* might…

But in the end it hadn't been Saul who had heard those shaming cries, who had seen…felt…*known* her body's urgent need for fulfilment.

She could feel her body starting to grow hot, and she had an urgent desire to run out of the building and away from Gareth Simmonds just as fast as she could. But of course she couldn't give in to such a childish temptation. Instead she held her head high and walked as calmly and quickly as she could towards the exit.

'I'll see you tonight,' Pam told her when the car stopped outside Louise's apartment building.

'Er…yes,' Louise agreed, before climbing out of the car.

Her telephone was ringing as she let herself into her apartment. Picking up the receiver, she was surprised to hear her twin's voice on the other end of the line.

Their mother's habits of good housekeeping and thriftiness had, as Katie had once ruefully confided to Louise, proved almost as beneficial in her career as her Oxford degree, her boss at the charity for whom she worked being profoundly impressed by Katie's firm grip on their departmental budget. As Louise was well aware, Katie was not given to making expensive overseas telephone calls merely for the self-indulgence of hearing her sister's voice.

Knowing this, her response to her twin's warm greeting was coloured by a little bit of anxiety as she asked her, 'What is it? Why are you ringing? Has something happened to Gramps or...?'

'No. Everything's fine.' Katie quickly reassured her. 'I just wanted to make sure you'd got back all right and that everything was...er...okay.'

There was a photograph of her sister, of both of them, in fact, in their university gowns, on the table just in sight of where Louise was standing, and she frowned suspiciously into her twin's smiling features now as she quickly mentally ran over all the various interpretations that could be put on Katie's comment.

'Why did you leave it until my flight to tell me Gareth Simmonds would be in Brussels?' she demanded quietly.

'I *wanted* to tell you,' Katie admitted guiltily. 'Don't be cross, Lou,' she coaxed. 'I just didn't want to spoil the weekend. Are you angry?'

Louise closed her eyes and then opened them again.

'What's to be angry about?' she asked as carelessly

as she could. 'With any luck I shan't have to have very much to do with him.

'How much longer are you working on your current project?' Louise asked her twin, firmly changing the subject and at the same time trying to banish from her mind the annoying image that would keep on forming there of Gareth's dark head inclined attentively towards Ilse's bright blonde one.

'I'm not quite sure,' she heard Katie telling her.

'Well, don't forget you promised you'd try to get over here soon if you can.'

'I will try,' Katie agreed. 'It was lovely seeing everyone at home—so much has happened while I've been away working in London that there was simply masses for me to catch up on with everyone. What with Tullah and Saul's new baby—and I couldn't get over how much Olivia and Caspar's two have grown—and Mum and Aunt Ruth have done wonders with their fund raising for their mums and babes. Mum told me that she and Aunt Ruth are going to try to buy an older house for conversion into flatlets for single mothers.

'Aunt Ruth was saying that the stable block at Queensmead would make a wonderful potential conversion, and that its setting would be perfect...'

'Gramps would never agree to anything like that,' Louise laughed, her face breaking into a wide grin as she pictured her irascible grandfather's reaction to the news that his sister wanted to turn the stable block of his large mansion into homes for the area's single mothers and their babies.

'No, I know, and so, of course, does Aunt Ruth. I sometimes suspect that the only reason she pretends to Gramps that she's serious about it is because she knows how much he loves to have something to get angry over and to fight about. He's just not been the same since Uncle David disappeared…'

'No. He hasn't,' Louise agreed, and for a second both of them were silent as they thought about their father's twin brother.

'Do you think we will *ever* hear anything from him again?' Katie asked Louise slowly, eventually.

'I don't know. I suspect that for Gramps's sake, if nothing else, Dad hopes that he will get in touch, and it must be strange, too, for Olivia. Her mother has another man in her life, and Olivia only sees her when she and Caspar go down to Brighton to stay with Olivia's grandparents. David doesn't even know that Caspar and Olivia are married, never mind that they've got two children.'

'I know… I can't imagine what it would be like not to have Mum and Dad, can you?' Katie asked.

'No. I can't,' Louise agreed.

Katie suddenly interrupted their discussion about their family life to ask her with unexpected urgency, 'Lou… It isn't bothering you *too* much… about…about Gareth Simmonds being there in Brussels is it?'

'No. Of course it isn't,' Louise denied. 'Obviously I would have preferred *not* to have had him working in the same arena, but because the Commission is so closely interwoven the fact that he *is* working here would have meant that we would have been bound to run into one another sooner or later, even if he hadn't been heading the same committee that Pam is on. After all, why *should* it bother me? I don't like him, it's true, but I can live with that.'

There were some things too private to discuss even

with someone as close to her as her twin was, and her real feelings about Gareth Simmonds and his presence in Brussels was quite definitely one of them.

'Look, I've got to go,' she told Katie. 'There's a big official dinner this evening, and I've got some reading up I need to do.'

These official Commission dinners, which in the early stages of her new job had filled her with such trepidation and seemed so daunting, had now become boringly familiar.

The dinner-table talk would be all the usual gossipy stuff, unleavened by anything genuinely worth talking about, Louise decided later, as she quickly showered and got herself ready, automatically pulling on the first of her wardrobe's three smart black dresses which she and Katie and Olivia had chosen on a weekend shop in London before Louise had taken up her new post.

The dresses, two of which had been bought as a bargain from a designer shop in Bond Street in its end-of-season sale, had more than paid for themselves, and in fact drew compliments every time she wore them. In matt black jersey, they were easy to wear and even more practical. They could actually be washed—a bonus indeed in view of the number of times Louise had to wear them. The one she had chosen to wear tonight was sleeveless, with a wide slashed neckline, the fabric fitting sleekly to her body and draping flatteringly over one hip.

Her urchin-short haircut needed little attention other than a fiercely expensive reshape every few weeks, and she had never favoured more than a minimal amount of make-up—eyeshadow in subtle smoky shades to emphasise the shape and depth of

her eyes, blusher, and lipstick which discreetly played
down the fullness of a mouth that caused members of
the male sex to stop and look again with speculative
interest.

Both she and Katie had inherited their father's lean,
elegant frame. Louise had never minded being tallish,
but she had on occasions during her teens wished that
her body was a little more curvaceously rounded.
Time had granted her that wish, and although she was
still enviably slender, according to her female friends,
she had the kind of distinctly feminine curves that
made the black jersey cling to her body with loving
fervour.

Black shoes and a handbag large enough to hold a
small notebook and a pen—things she never went
anywhere without—and she was ready, with five
minutes to spare before the car arrived.

Irritatingly her last thoughts as she stepped into the
waiting car were not of her recent conversation with
her twin, and Katie's promise to fly over to Brussels,
or even of the conversational pitfalls she might be
called upon to face regarding this morning's committee meeting at tonight's dinner, but instead were focused ominously and exclusively on the man who had
headed that committee meeting.

Gareth Simmonds. Hadn't she *already* wasted
enough, indeed far too much emotional energy on
him?

One of the first things she had done when she had
originally come here to Brussels to work was to tell
herself that she was not going to allow any events
from her past to cast dangerous shadows over her new
life—and one of the darkest and most dangerous shad-

ows in her life then had been the one cast by her ex-tutor…her ex…

Her head jerked up as she instinctively fought to deny even allowing herself to mentally frame the word 'lover'. They had *not* been lovers. Not in the true sense. Not as she interpreted the word.

Was there a woman in his life now? Pam, her boss, had made mention of the fact earlier that he was a single man, and as such would no doubt be in great demand socially.

'And not just single either,' Pam had commented admiringly. 'He's stunningly attractive and hunky with it…'

'Is he?' Louise had retorted in a clipped, short voice. 'I really hadn't noticed…'

Not noticed. When her brain had already faultlessly recorded and remembered the sheer thrill of female awe she had felt that first time she had seen him fully naked.

The car had stopped and the driver was, she realised belatedly, waiting for her to get out.

CHAPTER SIX

HOLDING her hand over her still half-full glass of wine, Louise shook her head at the circulating waiter, refusing his offer of a fresh glass.

It paid to keep a clear head at these affairs, and she had never been very good with alcohol.

Formal affairs such as this reception and the dinner which would follow it were really very much more Katie's strong suit than her own, and it had been brought very sharply home to her, not long after her original arrival in Brussels, that despite the fact that everyone close to her, including herself, always thought of *her* as being the stronger and more independently minded of the two of them it was Katie who had that nice degree of social confidence and easiness. She, as her twin, had developed the habit of allowing Katie to attend to all the social niceties that attended such conventional gatherings for *both* of them.

It had brought her rather sharply down to earth and humbled her a little to recognise how much she had depended on her twin in formal social situations, and indeed how much she had abused Katie's willingness to chat politely to ancient aunts, indeed to anyone whom she personally had deemed dull or boring, leaving her free to behave with unrepentant selfishness and very much please herself as to who she talked to and who she didn't.

A few months in Brussels had very quickly changed all that, and now Louise was adept at simulating interest in even the dullest of subjects—which didn't mean that she enjoyed it any more, she acknowledged ruefully as she directed a polite social smile towards the Commissioner paying her heavy compliments before excusing herself by saying that she thought her boss would be looking for her.

Louise made her way over to where Pam was deep in conversation with a fellow British Euro MP.

'Hello, Louise.' Pam welcomed her to her side.

'How is your aunt Ruth keeping, Louise?' the man Pam was in conversation with asked warmly. 'The last time I saw her she gave me the most fearful lecture on the damage she believes is threatening the British countryside from the volume of articulated lorries we're getting.'

Louise laughed. She knew John Lord quite well, since, in addition to being a Euro MP, he was also one of their close neighbours.

'Aunt Ruth is campaigning vigorously for a bypass for Haslewich, and she does have a point,' she conceded. 'The new business park outside the town *has* brought in an increased volume of traffic.

'I was just at home for the weekend, and my younger brother, Joss, was full of the fact that an Italian lorry driver had missed his road and got his artic stuck right in the middle of town, wedged solidly in between two listed buildings. Apparently it took the police five hours to unblock the traffic and get things back to normal.'

'It is a problem, I know,' John Lord agreed. 'The town does need a new bypass, and under one of the new EC agreements community funds should be provided to help pay for it.'

The conversation moved on and Louise excused

herself to go and circulate. It wouldn't do any harm to pick up as much feedback as she could after this morning's meeting.

Ten minutes later, just as she was discreetly checking her watch to find out how much longer it would be before they went in for dinner, she heard a familiar and very sensual voice behind her.

'Aha, there you are *chérie*...'

'Jean Claude.' She turned round immediately to smile up at him. He really was the most wickedly handsome-looking man, but oddly enough his almost film starish good looks did very little for her in any personal sense. Jean Claude was the kind of man who, while laying siege to one woman, would always be secretly looking over her shoulder to check out another potential victim. Louise suspected that her knowing this, realising that for him sex, seduction, relationships were all simply part of a very enjoyable but never serious game that he revelled in playing, automatically protected her, and prevented her from taking him too seriously.

'When are we going to get together?' he whispered to her as he skilfully drew her slightly away from everyone else. 'I have some leave owing to me. We could spend it together,' he suggested meaningfully. 'I could take you to Paris, show you things that only a person with experience could show you.'

Louise laughed and shook her head.

'Impossible, I'm afraid...'

'Ah, you are no doubt busy rushing to find laws to protect your cold northern seas. They are almost as cold as your heart, *chérie*...'

'And *both* are very well protected,' Louise informed him firmly, then smiled at him. This situation over fishing rights had never been one it was going to be easy to resolve, but she knew better than to respond to the lure that Jean Claude was trailing in front of her.

He might be a man who very much wanted to take her to bed, but he was also a Frenchman, with a vested interest in seeing his own country increase its allocation of the existing fishing rights. *She* wasn't powerful or important enough to influence the outcome of the newly formed committee in any shape or form, but it would be very easy for a woman who was emotionally vulnerable or not quite wary enough to be tricked into giving away information which *might* be useful to an opposing party, and Louise was very much aware of that fact.

Several yards away Gareth, who had been adroitly and very determinedly annexed by Ilse Weil virtually from the moment he'd arrived, frowned as he saw the way Jean Claude's hand lay possessively on Louise's arm, his body language making it plain that he would permit no other man to break into their intimate conversation.

Ilse, following his glance, raised her eyebrows.

'Oh, dear, I see Jean Claude is up to his tricks. It is well known here in Brussels what he is about,' she told Gareth with a dismissive shrug. 'And it is also rumoured that one of the reasons the French are so well informed is *because* of Jean Claude's skill in persuading his lovers to confide in him.'

She gave Gareth an arch look and made a purring sound deep in her throat as she told him, 'I'm afraid when *I'm* in bed with a man I lose myself so completely in the sex that the last thing *I* want to do is to talk politics…'

'I know what you mean,' Gareth agreed gravely. 'I too have a rule about never mixing business with pleasure…'

He was saved from having to say any more by an announcement requesting everyone to go in for dinner. Louise, he couldn't help noticing, seemed particularly reluctant to end her conversation with her companion.

'Louise.'

Louise tensed as she heard Gareth saying her name. The dinner had finished ten minutes ago, and she had hoped to slip away early, but now Gareth was bearing down on her, making it plain that he wasn't going to allow her to escape until he had said whatever it was he wanted to say to her.

'Gareth.' She acknowledged him curtly, glancing politely at her watch and then at the door.

'I saw you talking to Jean Claude le Brun earlier,' Gareth informed her, equally pointedly ignoring her attempts to show him that she was anxious to leave. 'You may not be aware of it, but it seems that he has something of a reputation in Brussels.'

Louise stared at him, her hackles immediately starting to rise as she caught the drift of Gareth's warning.

'A reputation for what?' she challenged him angrily. 'For being a good lover? What *is* it *exactly* you're trying to ask me, Gareth? Whether or not it's well deserved?'

'What I was trying to *warn* you against was the danger of putting yourself in a position where you

might inadvertently discuss certain sensitive subjects,'
Gareth corrected her grimly.

Louise's eyes widened and then darkened, first with
disbelief and then with anger, as she drew in a sharply
outraged breath.

'Are you *seriously* trying to suggest that Jean
Claude is trying to lure me into some kind of sex trap,
like…like someone out of a James Bond film?' she
demanded scornfully. 'How ridiculous and how *typi-cal* of you, Gareth. There *are* men who want to go to
bed with me simply for the pleasure of doing so,' she
informed him with angry scorn. 'They aren't all like
you, and—'

Abruptly she stopped, mentally cursing herself for
allowing her emotions to get the better of her. But it
was too late. Gareth had quite obviously heard her
and equally obviously wasn't going to let her escape.

'They aren't all like me and what?' he challenged
her silkily.

Furious with herself, and with him, Louise imme-diately took refuge behind the ploy of quickly chang-ing the subject.

'My private life has absolutely *nothing* whatsoever
to do with you,' she informed him, and then added
for good measure, 'You have no right, no right at all,
to dare to suggest to me that—' She broke off, and
then continued furiously, 'How would *you* like it if I
suggested to you that *you* should take care not to be
lured into bed by Ilse Weil? After all, *your* position
as head of the committee into the fisheries question
surely makes you far, *far* more vulnerable a target for
someone to try to influence your decision than me.'

She had a point, Gareth had to admit, but what he
couldn't admit—at least not to her—was the fact that

it wasn't merely concern for matters of diplomatic delicacy that had prompted his warning to her...

'You have no right to dictate to me *how* I live my private life,' Louise continued fiercely. 'You're not my tutor now, Gareth. You have *no* control over my life or my future. You might have been able to punish me for what you decided...for loving Saul, but—'

'To *punish* you?' Gareth interrupted her sharply. 'Louise, I promise you I—'

'You what?' she interrupted him shakily. 'You weren't responsible for the fact that I didn't get my first? It wasn't because of you that I—'

'You're not being fair.' He stopped her quietly. 'And neither are you being very logical. I wasn't your tutor and I—'

'No, you weren't,' Louise agreed. 'But...' She stopped. How could she admit to him that it had been because of her confused feelings for him, her fear of what those feelings actually were, that she hadn't been able to give her full attention to her work for her remaining time at university—that her thoughts of him had come between her and her work, that the sheer effort of denying them had drained her of the energy she needed for her study?

She was, she discovered, shamingly close to tears. The sheer intensity of the anger she was feeling was unblocking memories she had thought locked safely away.

Not once during her years at school had it occurred to her that she wouldn't always be the praised, clever student, and the shock to her pride and her self-esteem, never mind her plans for her future, when her work had been criticised had been very hard for her to come to terms with.

Yes, maybe *now*, with hindsight in a very small corner of her mind, she was just about beginning to admit that the life she was making for herself, the cut and thrust of the European scene, was far better suited to her passionate nature than the much more sterile atmosphere of the upper echelons of the British legal system would have been. But it was a very, very reluctant admission, and certainly not one she was prepared to share with Gareth Simmonds.

'I'm sorry if I said the wrong thing,' Gareth began quietly. 'I was simply trying to warn you.'

'Why warn me? What makes you think that *I'm* particularly in need of that kind of warning? Or can I guess? Just because I made the mistake of...of loving the wrong man...' She stopped and swallowed, and then told him bitingly, 'The relationship I choose to have with Jean Claude—*whatever* that relationship is—is no one's business but mine.'

'In one sense, no,' Gareth agreed. 'But in another... You don't need me to tell you that Brussels is a hotbed of gossip, and—'

'No, I don't,' Louise agreed tautly.

She had had enough of listening to Gareth lecture her. More than enough. Abruptly she turned on her heel, walking smartly away from him before he could say or do anything to stop her.

She was still seething over her run-in with him over an hour later, back in her flat, as she read through some notes while preparing for bed.

What right had he to dare to question the wisdom of her relationship with Jean Claude?

But it wasn't so much his assumed right to warn her that was making her so furiously angry—and not just with him but with herself as well—as the thinking she knew lay behind it. No doubt *he* was remembering her as the girl who had fallen so foolishly in love with a man who didn't want her, and who had then recklessly compounded her folly by inciting another man, who *also* didn't love her, to relieve her of her virginity—another man whom she had realised too late that she—

Those memories, that knowledge, and seeing Gareth, had reminded her of that hurt, and of her own foolishness.

Waking up early, unable to get back to sleep, Louise went down to the basement of the apartment complex which housed the gym and the swimming pool. At this hour of the morning she had the pool to herself, and the energy it took to make herself complete a punishing sixty lengths thankfully robbed her brain of the ability to concentrate on anything other than gritting her teeth and forcing herself to meet that target.

The last five lengths hadn't been a very sensible idea, she acknowledged when she eventually tried to haul herself out of the pool and discovered that she was too weak to do so. Instead she had to swim tiredly over to the steps and then climb them on legs that trembled with over-exertion and exhaustion.

Her short hair clinging sleekly to her scalp, her eyes momentarily closed as she willed herself not to give in to the jelly-like urging of her legs to simply sit down and rest, she was unaware of the fact that she was no longer alone in the pool area until she heard an unwontedly familiar voice demanding curtly, 'Louise? Are you all right...?'

Gareth Simmonds. What on earth was *he* doing here? Or was she simply hallucinating, dreaming him

up in some insane desire to inflict even further punishment upon herself?

Groggily she opened her eyes. No, she *wasn't*
dreaming. Despite the fact that the pool area was almost tropically heated, her skin suddenly broke out in
a rash of goosebumps, and she started visibly to
shiver. Gareth was standing less than a yard away
from her, wearing a pair of businesslike black swimming shorts. The rest of his body...

Louise swallowed and gulped, then tried to draw
extra oxygen into her suddenly starved lungs, a hot
flood of perspiration drenching her skin despite the
fact that she was actually trembling as though she was
icy cold.

The sight of him brought down an avalanche of
memories for which she was totally unprepared,
against which she had absolutely no defences, and she
could feel her knees starting to buckle under their
crushing weight.

In Tuscany he might have been more tanned, but
so far as she could see nothing else had changed. His
body was still the same male powerhouse of energy
and sensuality, and, yes, he *did* still have that same
arrowing of dark hair, so very masculine and dangerous to look at, but so soft and sensually stirring to
touch.

'Louise...'

She could feel the strength starting to leave her legs
as the blood roared in her head and her heart pounded
with sickening force.

'No.'

Automatically she put out a defensive hand as she
saw Gareth coming towards her, but he ignored it,
catching hold of her by the shoulders, his face, his

eyes, expressing an unexpected and unfamiliar look of concern as he demanded urgently, 'What is it? What's wrong? Are you feeling ill…?'

'Let…let me go,' Louise demanded, frantically struggling to pull herself free of his grip, but the tiled surround of the pool felt slippery beneath her wet feet, and she could feel herself starting to lose her balance, so that instead of pushing herself free of Gareth she had, instead, to cling onto him for security. This close she could smell the heat of his body—not, this time, as strongly musky as it had been on that fateful Tuscan day—and mingling with it a hint of lemon freshness from his soap…or aftershave…?

Louise wasn't even aware she had asked such a question until she heard him reply, his voice disconcertingly close to her ear, 'Shower gel. My eldest niece's choice—a Christmas present.'

'In Italy you smelled of…'

What was she saying…thinking…betraying…? She cursed herself mentally in desperation, but it was too late; Gareth was already holding her slightly away from him so that he could look down into her face, her eyes…

Louise blinked and tried to look away from him, but it was impossible. She felt her breath rattle in her lungs as their glances locked, clung, refusing to let go, like lovers' bodies.

'In Italy *you* smelled of sunshine and heat and of being a woman,' Gareth told her softly, as though he knew exactly what it was she had been about to betray herself by saying.

Louise opened her mouth to protest that what he was saying was wrong, that he was speaking the unspeakable, the unimaginable, the forbidden, but no words came out, and instead she discovered that she was focusing blindly on his mouth, studying it, staring at it as though she was starved for the...

'Louise...'

Afterwards she would ask herself why on earth her brain interpreted the way he said her name as an invitation to do what she did—to close the gap between them and to press her mouth against his, not so much in a kiss, more in a compulsive, instinctive response to a hunger that demanded far, far more than the mere meeting of their lips.

What she was doing was wrong, crazy...insane. But it was too late. She had already done it and Gareth... Gareth...

Heavily she closed her eyes as she heard him repeating her name over and over again, before he started to kiss her.

Her body trembled violently beneath his hands, but she made no move to stop him when he wrenched down the top of her swimsuit, baring her breasts to his touch. Against her body she could feel the hardness of his, and her own flesh leapt in immediate response, immediate recognition of its first...its *only* lover.

Heedlessly, ruthlessly, it laid waste to all the barriers she had painstakingly erected between herself and...and this... And instead of repudiating him, as she knew she must, Louise heard herself moaning his name, sobbing it aloud almost as she hung helplessly in his arms, her body no longer her own to command or protect, responsive only to what he might tell it or arouse within it.

She could feel the heat of his chest against the naked dampness of her breasts, and it was as though their first coming together had only been yesterday. As though she had learned *nothing* in the time since— as though all the resolutions she had made for herself in those long, agonising weeks and months afterwards, when she had finally realised just what was happening to her, just what *had* happened to her, had never been. As though this man had never caused her so much pain that she had sworn she would *never*, ever forget the agony of the lesson she had learned through him.

A sound, a long, tortured, aching sob of need and longing, tore at her throat. Beneath Gareth's hands she felt her body tremble and burn; beneath his mouth she felt herself melt, yield, yearn, until the intensity of her own hunger threatened to devour her.

All sense of place or time had long since left her. They could have been anywhere; she really didn't care. All that really mattered, all that was actually real, was what she could feel. Eagerly she pressed herself against Gareth, and felt the answering hardness in his own body.

Somewhere in the distance a door slammed, and abruptly Louise came back to reality. Immediately she pulled back from Gareth, covering her exposed breasts with her hands and then turning her back to him as she frantically struggled with the straps of her swimsuit.

'Louise.'

She could hear him saying her name urgently, but she shook her head in denial of whatever it was he might want to say to her, not even daring to turn round, knowing she couldn't allow herself to look at him as she denied him fiercely. 'No. No! Just leave me alone, Gareth… *leave me alone*.'

And without giving him the chance to stop her she started to walk away from him, and then to run.

Silently Gareth watched her go. What was there, after all, that he could say? What explanation, apology could he make for what he had done? To admit that he had momentarily lost control would make matters worse rather than better, and as for pointing out to her that she had been similarly vulnerable...

To see that tormented hurt in her eyes, to feel the need coursing through her body, to sense the longing she was so obviously struggling to repress and to know that she was repressing it because she still wanted, still loved another man, a man she could not have, had been like receiving a death blow, which was ironic when he had long ago assured himself—and believed those assurances—that he had come to terms with the knowledge that she loved someone else.

In Italy he had told himself initially that it had been anger, irritation, impatience with the way she was so wantonly and childishly destroying the pleasure of sharing herself with a partner who genuinely cared about her that had driven him to do what he had done. But he had known the moment he touched her that he was lying to himself, that he was just as guilty, just as burdened by inappropriate emotions for someone who did not want him as she was herself.

He might not have called those emotions love—not then—but he had known for sure what they were when he had held her in his arms and heard her cry out another man's name while *he* loved her.

Gareth closed his eyes. The Louise he had fallen in love with had been a mere girl, and he had derided himself for having done so, telling himself it was the classic tale of the mature tutor falling for his youthful pupil, hoping to recapture his own youth through her. But they were tutor and pupil no longer, and Louise was now a woman in *every* sense of the word. And his feelings hadn't changed, merely deepened, strengthened. But then he hadn't needed anyone to tell him that. He had known it the moment he saw her on the plane. Had known it even before then.

Had known it at Christmas, when his family had teased him about his lack of a wife and children of his own. Had known it and ached for it as he'd held his youngest nephew in his arms and known beyond any kind of doubt that the only mother he wanted for *his* children was Louise. How had it happened? He didn't know. And when? Before Italy? What did it matter now? All that mattered was that quite obviously for Louise nothing had changed, and she still loved her cousin Saul.

Even though she had had a hot shower to warm her cold body, and drunk a mug of coffee, she was still shivering, still shaking with reaction to what had happened down by the pool, Louise acknowledged. And no amount of water, no matter how piping hot, could wash away the scent of Gareth that still clung somehow to her own skin, which had embedded itself for ever in her vulnerable senses.

Gareth.

When had she known just how she really felt about him? In Italy, when she had fought to deny it with a ferocity that should have warned her just how frightened she really was? At home that Christmas when everyone had tiptoed around her, afraid of mentioning

Saul's name or the fact that he and Tullah had now
set a date for their marriage, when in reality Saul and
what she had once felt for him had paled to the
faintest of shadows?

Gareth.

She had denied for as long as she could what had
happened to her, telling herself that she was just over-
reacting, that it was the classic virgin's response to
her first experience of sex to imagine she was in love
with the man who had been her partner, reminding
herself with bitter scorn of how pathetically trite it
was for a student to fall in love with her tutor.

You don't even like him, she had told herself over
and over again. You're just transferring your feelings
to him from Saul… He doesn't really mean anything
to you, and you certainly don't mean *anything* to *him*.

The last part of that statement might have been true
but the rest of it certainly hadn't.

And so she had transferred to another course, had
told herself bitterly that she was *glad* that Gareth no
longer taught her, had done everything and *anything*
she could to make sure that she never came into contact with him. But, while she might have been able to
control her daytime waking thoughts and responses,
at night in her dreams it had been different. At night
in her dreams she'd ached for him, yearned for him,
clung to him while her body desperately tried to relive
the pleasure he had given it.

The pain, the agony of waking each morning to the
reality of knowing that he didn't want her, that he
wasn't a part of her life, had shown her more clearly
than anything else just how childish and adolescent
her feelings for Saul had actually been.

With Gareth there had been no question of her try-

ing to pursue him, to convince him that he really
wanted and loved her, no adolescent fantasising that
against all the evidence to the contrary she could
make him love her.

Finally, she had grown up.

She was still shivering, and her head had started to
pound with sick intensity, a sure sign that she was
about to suffer one of her fortunately rare migraine
attacks. It was pointless even thinking about trying to
go to work. Dizzily she picked up the phone and di-
alled her boss's number.

'A migraine!' Pam exclaimed when she had explained how she felt. 'Don't even *think* of trying to
come into work. I know how bad they can be.'

By now the pain was so intense that it was all
Louise could do to croak a disjointed response before
she replaced the receiver and somehow managed to
drag herself into her bedroom.

Gareth Simmonds. Why had fate so cruelly brought
him back into her life? Why?

CHAPTER SEVEN

LOUISE woke up abruptly. Her migraine had gone and someone was knocking very loudly and impatiently on her apartment door. Pushing back the bedclothes, she swung her legs onto the floor, grimacing as she realised she had gone to bed still wearing her swimsuit.

As always in the aftermath of one of her migraines, she felt mercifully pain-free, but somehow slightly unfocused and not quite together, her body and her brain both working slowly as she reacted automatically to the continued knocking and went to open the door.

'Joss! Jack! What on earth are you two doing here?' she exclaimed as she saw her younger brother and cousin.

Whoever she had expected to find outside her door it had certainly not been them.

'Lou, Jack isn't feeling very well,' her brother announced urgently, ignoring her question as he put a comforting, protective arm around his cousin's shoulders and ushered him into Louise's apartment.

'He was sick during the Channel crossing and...'
'Sick...'

As Louise inspected the slightly green and heavyeyed face of her younger cousin she recognised that he was indeed looking extremely unwell.

'Jack...' she began in concern.

But he shook his head and told her wanly, 'I'll be fine... I just need to lie down for a while...'

'The bedroom's this way, Joss,' Louise informed her brother, leading the way as Joss guided his cousin across her small living room and into the inner hallway that gave on to the apartment's single bedroom.

Quickly straightening the bed before Jack virtually fell down on top of it, Louise frowned. What on earth were the two boys doing here?

Jack, Olivia's younger brother, had made his home permanently with Louise's parents following his father's disappearance some years earlier, and was now looked upon by Louise as more of another brother than a cousin.

His mother, never particularly maternal and suffering from an eating disorder, had announced that the last thing she felt capable of doing was single-handedly looking after a teenage boy—and one, moreover, who had already spent far more of his time with her brother-in-law and his wife than he had with her—and Olivia, his elder sister, while more than willing to give him a permanent home, had allowed herself to be persuaded by Jenny and Jon that it was in Jack's best interests for him to remain where he was, living under their roof, instead of being subjected to even more changes.

It was an arrangement which worked very well. At fourteen, Joss was two years younger than Jack, and they were not just close in age but close in other ways as well—more so than if they had actually been brothers, Jenny often said. And to Louise and Katie, growing up in their parents' comfortable family home, Jack had simply been accepted as though he were an extra sibling.

There had been some talk of Jack going to Brighton to live with his mother and his maternal grandparents once his mother's health had recovered, but when offered this option Jack had declared very firmly that he wanted to stay where he was.

An extra mouth to feed, an extra child to love and nurture was, as Louise knew, no problem to her parents, and if anyone had ever asked her she herself would have said quite honestly that she'd never thought of Jack as being anything other than a very close member of her intimate family, and she knew that her twin would have said exactly the same.

Within the family Joss and Jack were known collectively as 'the boys', just as she and Katie were referred to as 'the twins', but she hadn't missed the way that Jack had withdrawn from her just now, when she had gone to give him the same swift and automatic hug of greeting she had given to Joss, nor the way he hunched his body away from her as he lay on her bed as though somehow in rejection of her.

As she closed her bedroom door she beckoned to her brother to follow her into her small kitchen, where she automatically filled the kettle with water and, much to her own wry amusement, heard herself taking on a role which she had hitherto assumed belonged exclusively to women like her mother as she asked him, 'Are you hungry. I don't have much in, but I can rustle up some sandwiches, I expect.' And then, without waiting for a response, she continued firmly, 'What on earth is going on, Joss? What are you doing here? Mum never rang to say you were coming. I don't even have a spare room to—'

'Mum doesn't know.'

Louise, who had been just about to start slicing

some bread to make him some sandwiches, stopped what she was doing and turned to face him, putting the knife down on the breadboard.

'What do you mean, Mum doesn't know?' she demanded suspiciously. There was a small silence while her brother looked down at his feet and then at the kitchen wall.

'That's one of the sketches you did in Tuscany, isn't it?' he asked her. 'I—'

'Joss.' Louise warned him.

'I've left them a note...explaining.'

Louise's eyebrows rose.

'Explaining what?' she asked warily.

'Well, I couldn't tell them what we were doing— they would have stopped us.'

'Oh, now, surely not,' Louise protested dryly. 'I mean, why on earth should she? You're only fourteen. I can't think of any reason on earth why the parents should possibly object to the pair of you doing a disappearing act...'

Joss gave her a sheepish look.

'I know. I know...' he conceded. 'But I had to come. If I hadn't...I tried to persuade Jack that it wasn't a good idea, but he just wouldn't listen, and the mood he was in I was afraid he would just up and leave anyway. At least this way I was able to come with him and persuade him that we should come here to you. He didn't want to, and it took me ages to persuade him that you might be able to help...'

'To help with what?' Louise demanded, exasperated.

'He wants to find David...his father,' Joss told her simply.

There was a brief silence while brother and sister

looked at one another, and then Louise picked up the bread knife and reached for the loaf, telling Joss quietly, 'I think you'd better tell me the whole story.'

Ten minutes later, when she and Joss were sitting opposite one another in the small sitting room, Joss biting appreciatively into the sandwiches she had just made, he told her with a grin, 'Do you know, you sounded just like Mum back there in the kitchen?'

He was growing up fast, Louise recognised as she studied his lanky frame. Once he filled out a bit more he would probably top Max's six-foot frame, and maybe even grow taller than the Chester cousins, the shortest of whom was a good six feet two.

'Mmm...maybe. But don't expect me to listen as indulgently to whatever piece of mischief the pair of you are up to as she would,' Louise warned him, adding, 'You're lucky I was here. I *should* have been at work. If I hadn't had to go back to bed this morning with a migraine...'

'Yes, it was lucky,' Joss agreed, happily munching on another sandwich. 'I *was* a bit worried about how I was going to persuade Jack to hang around if you weren't here. When we hitched a lift from the ferry terminal he was all for going as far as Spain before we stopped.'

'Spain?'

'Mmm...He said that Uncle David once sent Gramps a card from there. Jack saw it when he went round. It was on Gramps' desk, apparently, although he couldn't get a proper look at it, and he says that when he went back to try and read it *properly* it had gone.'

'To read it *properly*? He had no right to be even thinking of doing such a thing,' Louise told him severely, wisely forgetting all the times she had been guilty of attempting to read her school reports upside down on her father's desk.

'Uncle David *is* his father,' Joss pointed out with unanswerable logic.

'Yes. I know,' Louise agreed. She started to frown. What she had initially assumed was just some boyish prank was beginning to take on a much more ominous perspective. So far as she knew, Jack had been happy—very happy—to make his home with her parents. She couldn't remember ever having heard him *mention* his father, never mind expressing a desire to see him. Olivia, she knew, had very ambiguous feelings about both her parents, and had once remarked to her that she found it was much, much easier to think charitably of them now that they were not a part of her day-to-day life.

'I know that Uncle David is Jack's father,' Louise repeated. 'What I *don't* understand is why Jack should have decided he needs to see him so urgently that the pair of you have to set out to do so without first discussing it with Mum and Dad. Has there been a problem at home—a row about something…bedrooms not being kept tidy, homework not being done, that kind of thing?' Louise asked, mentally casting her mind back to her own adolescence and the areas of contention between herself and her parents then that might have led to her taking the same kind of action. Although, to be fair, she couldn't actually remember ever having wanted to leave home.

'No, it's nothing like that.' Joss shook his head, his answer so immediate and so positive that Louise knew he was telling her the truth.

'Then what *is* it?' she asked him.

'Not what, but *who*...' Joss corrected her, explaining, 'It's Max. He was in a foul mood when he was home last time. I think he must have quarrelled with Maddy because I saw her crying in the kitchen. Max had wanted Dad to play golf with him, but Dad said he couldn't because he'd already promised to take Jack fishing. Max probably wanted to borrow money off him anyway—you know what he's like.'

'Go on,' Louise encouraged him when he paused to wolf down the last of the sandwiches. She would have to go out and buy some extra food. There was no way she had enough in her meagre store cupboards to fuel a pair of appetites like her brother's and her cousin's.

'Well, I don't know exactly what Max did say to Jack, but...' Joss pulled a face. 'All Jack would say was that Max had called him a cuckoo in the nest, unwanted by his own parents, and asked Jack if he had any idea how much his school fees were costing Dad. Not that it's—'

'He did *what*? Do the parents know about any of this?' Louise asked her brother acerbically.

Joss shook his head. 'No. I wanted to tell them but Jack wouldn't let me. I think he's a bit afraid that Max might be right and that—'

'Right? Of course he isn't right. Mum and Dad look on Jack as one of us,' Louise protested indignantly. 'They'd no more begrudge the cost of Jack's school fees than they would yours. Less...'

'No, I know that. But you know how Max is about money...'

'Yes. I do know,' Louise agreed. It was an unfathomable mystery to her how she and the rest of her siblings, her cousins, could ever have come from the same gene pool as Max.

'I suppose one of the things that makes Max so horrid is that, deep down inside, he must know that no one likes him,' Joss suggested.

Louise gave him a surprised look.

'If only! If you're trying to drum up my sympathy for Max you're wasting your time—and putting the cart before the horse. The reason no one likes *Max* is because he is the way he is, not the other way around. Look at the way he treats poor Maddy—'

Louise broke off, wondering belatedly if her mother would approve of her discussing such a subject with her younger sibling. But Joss didn't look in the least disconcerted by her comment.

'Aunt Ruth says that Maddy is a bit like a sleeping beauty, and that she doesn't do anything because she hasn't woken up to her own true potential yet. Aunt Ruth says one day she will, and that when she does Max had better watch out,' Joss told her simply.

'Jack says that he doesn't want to be a burden on the parents any longer,' he added, 'and that he intends to find his father and make him repay Dad for everything that he's spent on him. *And* he says that if he can't then he'll have to forget about university and get a job so that he can earn some money to repay them himself...'

'Oh, Joss,' Louise protested emotionally. 'That's the last thing Dad or Mum would want him to do. Why on *earth* didn't he talk to them about this instead of...?'

'He said he couldn't because he knew that they would deny everything,' Joss told her.

'They would deny it because it simply isn't true.

They love him just as much as any of us,' Louise protested.

'I *know* that,' Joss agreed. 'But I don't think that Jack does. It must be hard for him, though, because in a way Max was right about one thing. Uncle David and Aunt Tania didn't really want him and Olivia... Not like Mum and Dad want us.'

Louise bowed her head, knowing that there was nothing she could say.

'Different people have different ways of loving,' she informed her brother gruffly. 'Just because Uncle David and Aunt Tania weren't as good at parenting as the folks, that doesn't mean that Olivia and Jack weren't loved and wanted.'

Joss looked steadily at her. 'Aunt Ruth says that having truly loving parents is like having a hundred fairy godmothers—only better!'

Louise gave her brother an old-fashioned look.

'All right, now I know why Jack is so determined to find his father—although how on earth he hopes to do so when Dad's tried without success I *don't* know. But what I don't fully understand is exactly what *you* are doing with him...'

'I couldn't let him go on his own,' he told her simply. 'Anything could have happened to him. So I thought if I could persuade him to stop off here with you, you could...'

'I could *what*?' Louise prompted, firmly ignoring the sharp tug of emotion she had felt as she listened to him. Her brother had enough admiring fans already without her adding herself to the list.

'Well, I told Jack that you might be able to find something out for him...what with Brussels being the headquarters of the European Union and everything, but...'

'I understand what you're saying, Joss,' Louise agreed. 'But you do know, don't you, that Mum and Dad will *have* to be told where you are, and that they'll insist that the pair of you go straight back to school?'

'Yes, I know.'

Louise looked at him. She had a pretty shrewd suspicion that Joss had known exactly what would happen in stopping off to see her, *and* she suspected that he had deliberately manipulated events so that a full stop would be placed on Jack's expedition before it took them too far from home.

'You stay here with Jack,' she told him. 'I need to go out and do some shopping if I'm going to be able to feed you. When I come back I think a telephone call to home would be in order, don't you?'

Gareth paused in the foyer to the apartment block. He had had to call in to see Pam Carlisle earlier in the day, to check on a couple of points she had raised in the committee, and during the course of their conversation she had happened to mention that Louise had been struck down with a bad migraine. He would be the last person she would feel like seeing. He knew that, especially after this morning. But it hadn't been difficult getting her apartment number from her boss, though he had to admit he had felt a small stab of guilt over the way he had described himself to her as an old friend of the family.

'Oh, really? Louise never said,' she had responded, obviously rather puzzled.

'It probably slipped her mind,' Gareth had responded.

No, *she* wouldn't want to see *him*, but he wanted...*needed* to see her. This morning... He closed his eyes. Damn it, his body still ached unbearably for her, but that was *nothing* compared with the agony of deprivation and loss that was affecting his emotions.

Joss answered the door to his knock, recognising him straight away and welcoming him in.

'Louise's just gone out for reinforcements... food...' he explained with a warm smile.

'I was just going to make a cup of tea for Jack,' he explained as he led the way to Louise's small kitchen. 'He didn't feel very well on the ferry and he's lying down. Can I make one for you?'

Gareth smiled his acceptance, his attention briefly caught by Louise's sketch of Tuscany.

'Louise drew it,' Joss remarked as Gareth studied the sketch of the small shrine on the road to his family's villa.

'Yes,' Gareth agreed, without removing his attention from the sketch.

'She's not the world's best artist,' Joss elaborated. 'Strictly speaking her perspective could be improved upon.'

'Strictly speaking,' Gareth agreed urbanely.

'But of course I expect *you* see it with rather different eyes,' Joss commented simply.

Gareth swung round to look properly at him.

He had got to know Louise's family well during the summer in Tuscany. Joss had been rather younger then, of course, but Gareth had very quickly picked up on the fact that within his family he already had the reputation of being something of a prophet and a seer, and was blessed with, if not exactly foresight, then certainly twenty-twenty emotional vision. Bearing in mind all this, Gareth resisted the temptation to probe more deeply into the reasoning behind his statement and said calmly instead, 'Yes. I believe I do. Are you and Jack planning a long stay with your sister?' he asked conversationally, determinedly changing the subject.

'Er...no... The thing is, she wasn't *really* expecting us at all. She's only got one bedroom...'

Gareth had enough experience from dealing with his nieces and nephews, not to mention his students, to know when someone was being evasive, and it wasn't very long before he had managed to coax the full story out of Joss.

'What makes Jack believe his father might be found in Spain?' he asked him, when he had finished.

Half an hour later, when Louise eventually returned to the apartment, weighed down by several bulging carrier bags, it was to discover that not only had Gareth apparently made himself very much at home in her apartment, but that it had additionally been arranged that her brother and her cousin were going to be staying with him, and not, after all, with her.

'Gareth says he doesn't mind, and since he's got a spare bedroom it seemed the sensible thing to do,' Joss informed her as the three of them deftly relieved her of her heavy shopping.

On the point of informing Gareth in no uncertain terms that there was absolutely no need for him to involve himself in what, after all, was a purely personal family affair, Louise looked across her small and now very crowded sitting room, which seemed to be filled with very big males, and hesitated.

'I promise you, they'll be perfectly safe,' Gareth informed her quietly.

Louise frowned as she looked from his clear, intent gaze to her brother and then her cousin who was now out of bed and looking better, correctly interpreting the message both in Gareth's words and his expression that he knew what was going on.

While she had been rushing round the supermarket snatching up food she had acknowledged that the first thing she needed to do was to speak to her parents—something it would be very difficult for her to do with Jack in the apartment with her. If Gareth took both boys back to *his* apartment with him she would at least have the opportunity to speak openly to her mother and father, and she knew, too, that they would both be safe in Gareth's hands, that she need not worry that he would somehow allow Jack to do a disappearing act on them. In fact, if she was honest, it was almost a relief to have Gareth there, if not to take charge then certainly to play a supporting role in the small mini-drama which had erupted into her life.

A relief to have *Gareth* there? She could feel herself starting to stiffen with inner apprehension at the thought, but oddly, instead of telling him that his help most certainly wasn't needed, she found herself turning instead to Jack and asking him gently, 'Are you feeling okay now?'

'Yes,' he responded. 'It was the ferry and then the jolting of the lorry ride…it made me feel really sick.'

'I told you you shouldn't have eaten that curry,' Joss remarked severely.

'I was hungry,' Jack countered. 'And anyway, *I*

wanted to go straight to Spain, not come here first and—'

'Look, why don't we argue out the pros and cons of this later?' Gareth interposed, pushing back his sleeve to look at his watch as he announced, 'It's almost six p.m., and I don't know about everyone else, but I'm getting hungry. What do you say to you two coming round to my flat with me, where you can have a shower and get yourselves sorted out, and then, say at seven o'clock, we'll come back for Louise and the four of us can go out for something to eat?'

Louise opened her mouth to object, to say that she was perfectly capable of making her own arrangements, not just for the boys' welfare but for her own supper as well, but quite unaccountably she discovered that she was closing it again without a word of protest being uttered.

Both boys had brought haversacks with them, and with truly amazing speed Gareth soon had them and their belongings organised and marshalled at the door of her apartment.

'Is seven o'clock all right for you?' he asked Louise as Joss opened the door.

'Yes...it's...it's fine,' she agreed. The close confined space of her small hallway made it impossible for her to move away from him. Was it really only this morning that he had held her in his arms and she had...? Shakily she closed her eyes, unable to bear the burden of the memories she was reliving.

'Are you all right? Is it your migraine...?'

Her *migraine*... How did *he* know about that?

Louise's eyes opened abruptly.

'I'm fine,' she told him curtly. How would it feel to be the woman Gareth loved, the woman he wanted to cherish and protect, to spend his life with, to have his children with? She could feel herself starting to tremble deep down inside, and it was several minutes after they had gone before she felt able to walk to the telephone and dial her parents' telephone number.

Her mother answered the phone almost immediately, and Louise could hear the anxiety in her voice as she did so.

'It's all right, Mum ,' she told her quickly. 'They're here with me.'

'They're *what*?' She could hear the astonishment in her mother's voice. 'But what...? Why...?'

Quietly Louise outlined the details of the story Joss had told her.

'Oh, no,' her mother protested when she had finished. 'I can't believe that Jack could ever think we felt like that. Neither your father nor I have ever...' Her mother stopped speaking for a moment as her emotions overwhelmed her.

'And you say Joss told you that it's because of what Max said to him that Jack has decided that he's being a burden on us...?'

'Well, yes, at least according to Joss. But I was wondering, Mum...' Louise paused and nibbled thoughtfully on her bottom lip. 'He's at a very sensitive age, and no matter how much you and Dad love him you *aren't* his mother and father. There are bound to be times when he wonders about them, when he feels angry and hurt and rejected by what they've done, and perhaps...'

'Yes. I understand what you're saying,' her mother agreed quietly. 'Olivia and Ruth both think that we...that all of us might have been over-compensating to him for the fact that David and Tania aren't here, and I think they're probably right. Thank goodness Joss had the good sense to come to you...'

'Mmm...' Louise agreed, and then added warningly. 'I don't want to sound pessimistic, but it seems to me that this isn't something that's going to go away very easily. All right, *this* time he's here, but...'

'I know what you mean,' her mother acknowledged swiftly. 'And it isn't even a matter of ensuring that he doesn't take off to go looking for his father again. There are quite obviously some very important issues concerning his parents troubling Jack. Issues which he no doubt thinks can only be resolved by discussing them with his father face to face. Right now Jack needs David, and I only wish it was possible for him to have him here. Since he disappeared your father has tried very hard to trace him, but without any success. Your grandfather has received the odd card from him, just telling him that he's safe, but that's all. Where are the boys now, by the way?' her mother asked.

Louise hesitated.

'Well, actually, they're with Gareth Simmonds,' she told her, trying to sound as casual as she could, but horridly aware that her voice sounded just a little too high-pitched and strained. 'You remember him, don't you, Mum? He was in Tuscany when—'

'Gareth? Of *course* I remember him,' her mother agreed. 'Katie said that he was working in Brussels, and I wondered if the two of you would bump into one another.'

'Well, he has an apartment in the same block as me, and since he has a spare bedroom, and I don't, he's offered to put the boys up there. I was glad, really, because it's given me an opportunity to ring you and speak to you without Jack being here. You'll have to let me know what arrangements you want me to make for sending them home—always supposing that Jack can be *persuaded* to go home voluntarily...'

'Mmm. I know that could be tricky. Look, let me speak to your father, and to Olivia as well. After all, Jack is her brother. Can I ring you back later?'

'Yes, that would be a good idea. Gareth and the boys are coming round for me at seven, and we're going out for something to eat.'

'Well, give them both our love, and thank Gareth on our behalf for being so helpful, will you, please, Lou?' her mother asked, before ringing off.

Thank Gareth for being so *helpful*. Oh, yes, and perhaps her mother would like her to fling herself into his arms and give him a big kiss as well...

Involuntarily Louise discovered that she was curling her toes into her shoes, her whole body threatening to tremble with aching longing.

It had been several years now since she had forced herself to make a constructive critical analysis of herself and to recognise certain self-destructive personality traits, chief among which had to be her self-willed stubbornness—the stubbornness which had kept her locked in the belief that her teenage crush on Saul was the kind of love that made them matched soulmates and him the only man she could ever love or want.

By the time she had learned that real love was a far more complex and sometimes less easily recognised emotion it had been too late. The damage had been done.

Now, with the benefit of hindsight, it seemed incredible to her that she had never stopped to question

just why she had been so determined, so eager, to go
to bed with Gareth. Simply to shed the burden of her
virginity? No! Oh, no. Somewhere all along, even
though she had refused to recognise or acknowledge
it at the time, among the anger, the resentment, the
sense of furious anguished pain, there had been something else, something which had not merely been sexual curiosity or even physical attraction.

It hurt her to acknowledge even in the privacy of
her own most secret thoughts that a part of her had
wanted, needed, ached for Gareth all along—for
Gareth himself, not just as a substitute, any substitute,
for the intimacy she'd been denied with Saul. And of
course Gareth himself must surely, at some level, have
recognised that fact—he was, she suspected, far too
intelligent not to have done so, which no doubt explained why he had been only too pleased for her to
distance herself from him.

After all she had learned from her unwanted pursuit
of Saul, she had been proudly determined she was not
going to repeat that mistake with Gareth. She was not
going to offer her love, *herself*, and be rejected—but
oh, how she had ached for him to want her, to love
her, and to show and tell her so. Stupid, impossible
dreams of course!

'Gareth telephoned…' her mother had said, shortly
after their return from Italy, and her heart had stood
still while she fought to stop her body's physical reactions from betraying what she was feeling, from
giving away any trace of that huge, weakening surge
of need and longing that had swept over her.

'Mmm…' her mother had continued. 'He'd heard
from Maria that we'd been called back unexpectedly,

and he was just ringing to see if everything was all right...'

To see if everything was all right... Not to see if *she* was all right, not to speak to her...not to say, to ask... Fiercely she had swallowed back her tears, clenching her hands into tight fists.

Please God, not again...not a second time. This time she was not going to make a fool of herself by showing her feelings... This time...this time she was a woman, Louise had recognised painfully. This time she was not going to cry for a man who didn't want her, like a child crying for a denied need. This time she wasn't even going to let herself acknowledge her feelings. What feelings? She had no feelings—at least not where Gareth Simmonds was concerned. Why should she have? After all, he had no feelings for her!

'Anyone want more coffee?'

To Louise's initial chagrin, it had been Gareth who proved to be the more knowledgeable about the city's restaurants, despite the fact that she had lived there for much longer.

'I'm only going on what I've been told,' he had volunteered when Louise hadn't quite been able to conceal her reaction to his expertise.

The square where they had eaten was surrounded by streets on which fish vendors and restaurants displayed their wares on open stalls.

Predictably, it had been the more visually unappealing species of fish—to Louise's eye at least—which had caught the boys' enthusiastic attention.

'Ugh...it looks horrid,' Louise had objected when Joss had drawn her attention to a particularly vicious-looking glassy-eyed monster.

'Mmm... I don't know whether or not it's a sign of getting old, but I must say that these days I prefer not to be able to recognise the food on my plate in its original life form,' Gareth had calmly responded to the boys when they had derided her for her squea-mishness. But Louise had been ruefully amused to notice that neither of the boys had taken the restau-rateur up on his offer to go and choose their fish as they swam in their tanks.

The streets around the square were busy and bus-tling, creating an almost holiday-like atmosphere—which must be the reason she was feeling so danger-ously happy, Louise decided as both boys declared themselves satisfactorily full in response to Gareth's question.

The ambience of the square was one of relaxed en-joyment and a warmth that one might more readily have associated with Paris rather than Brussels, with its unfairly 'staid burgher' reputation. Because of its present-day association with the Common Market and modern politics, one sometimes forgot that Brussels was a city with a long and distinguished history.

Louise also shook her head in response to Gareth's offer of more coffee. The evening had gone surpris-ingly well. It had amazed and, yes, if she was honest, piqued her just a little to see how quickly Gareth had re-established a very strong rapport with both her brother and her cousin.

Of the four of them she was probably the one who felt the most self-conscious and wary, she recognised, and that was because... She bent down to reach for her purse, determined to ensure that she paid for her own and the boys' meal.

There had been moments during the evening when

she had found herself joining in with the boys' laughter as Gareth told them a particularly funny story about his own family, but her laughter had quickly been replaced by a feeling of envious sadness. *She* would never be a part of his life. *She* would never be special to him, as his sisters and his nieces and nephews so obviously were. He would *never* love her the way he loved them; his eyes would *never* light up warmly when he spoke of her, thought of her. If he had cared he would never have ignored what had happened between them—and ignored her!

'Well, if everyone's ready, I think we'd better be going,' Gareth announced as he glanced at his watch.

To Louise's relief he made no objection to her statement that she intended to pay their bill.

Jack, she was relieved to see, was looking much happier than he had done at the beginning of the evening. Louise ached to be able to reassure him that whatever Max had said to him, however hurtful it must have been, could never be a true reflection of what the other members of their family felt, but she could sense that he would close up on her if she did, and that he was still feeling too sensitive for the subject to be easily broached. And besides, she guessed intuitively, it wasn't so much *her* reassurance he craved and needed, nor even that of her parents, but rather that of his own parents, and most especially his father.

As they left the restaurant Louise discovered that the boys were walking ahead of her while Gareth fell into step beside her. Instinctively she started to walk a little bit faster, but Gareth kept pace with her. In her haste to make sure that she wasn't left on her own with him, she almost stumbled.

Immediately Gareth's hand shot out to steady her, his body offering a bulwark for her to lean into while she got her balance. Weakly Louise closed her eyes. The evening air was heavy with the scent of the traffic and the city, but stronger by far was her awareness of the sensual warmth of Gareth's body, its scent dizzying her, robbing her of the ability to fight her desire to move closer to him, her illusion that he *wanted* her to move closer.

To her chagrin she discovered that her hand was resting against his chest. No, *clinging* almost to his jacket, she recognised, her head inclining helplessly towards his shoulder.

'Are you all right? Your migraine hasn't come back, has it?' she heard him asking her, his voice almost short and terse, as though... As though he was uncomfortable with the way she was practically leaning against him, Louise decided. But when she struggled to pull herself away he wouldn't let her. The boys had stopped several yards ahead of them to study a sculpture in the centre of the small square they were walking through, their faces absorbed.

'It must have been a shock for you to have the pair of them turn up on your doorstep so unexpectedly,' she heard Gareth saying to her as she weakly allowed herself to relax back into the warmth of his body, and the arm he had placed so securely around her. 'I must say I think you've handled the situation very well.'

'Er...thanks for stepping in the way you did,' Louise responded. 'My parents said to give you their thanks as well, by the way. I spoke to my mother after you'd gone. She's going to ring me back later to discuss what arrangements they're going to make to get the boys home...' She paused, and looked worriedly across at her brother and her cousin.

'Has...? Did...? Jack wants to find his father...and—'

'Yes, I know.' Gareth interrupted her gently. 'I take it that no one does know where he is?'

'Dad's tried to find him,' Louise told him, 'but without any success. Oh, I could wring Max's neck. He must have *known* how upset Jack would be by what he said. He really is the most selfish, thoughtless...'

'Unlike the rest of his family, who, from what *I've* seen of them, are extremely caring and concerned for one another,' Gareth told her.

It was impossible for her to see his expression properly now that it was dark, but Louise could hear an intensity of emotion in his voice that surprised her.

Gareth looked down at the top of her head. Protecting one another obviously came easily and naturally to most members of the Crighton family.

He could still remember how determined to protect her twin her sister Katie had been, when she had explained to him just why Louise was skipping so many lectures.

'Louise...about this morning...'

Immediately he could feel her tensing, and starting to withdraw from him.

'I don't want to talk about it,' she told him quickly. 'I...it shouldn't have happened. I...'

Cursing himself under his breath, Gareth immediately let her go. What a fool he was. Just because for a few moments she had relaxed in his arms, that didn't mean... Mind you, he derided himself inwardly, it was probably just as well she *had* put some distance between them. Another few seconds of standing close to her like that and she would surely have discovered exactly what kind of effect she was having on him.

He saw the way she was studying Joss and Jack and, guessing what she was thinking, tried to comfort her.

'Try not to worry,' he advised her. 'I'm sure your parents will find some way to reassure him.'

'I hope so,' she agreed. 'But they can't…they aren't… I was thinking earlier, when we were in the restaurant…trying to imagine how *I* would feel if I were Jack. It must be hard for him, and I can understand *why* he would want to find Uncle David.'

'Yes,' Gareth agreed quietly, 'but there are other, more effective ways of doing so than giving up his studies and hitch-hiking all over Europe…as I'm sure your father will be able to explain to him.'

It was an odd and very disconcerting experience to have Gareth trying to comfort her instead of criticising her. Somehow it had been a lot easier to try to cope with her feelings when they were antagonists.

At Gareth's insistence he and the boys saw her back to her own apartment, and Gareth even insisted that she open the door and go inside before they left her.

Impulsively Louise turned to hug first her brother and then Jack.

'Thanks for everything, Lou,' he told her gruffly, returning her hug with teenage embarrassment.

'There's nothing to thank me for,' Louise told him, ruffling his hair. 'You're my…you're family.'

Quickly blinking back the tears she knew he would be embarrassed to see, she turned to thank Gareth once again for his help, and then gasped back a small sound of shock, as instead of keeping his distance from her, he was actually taking her in his arms and hugging her just as fiercely as Jack had done. But the sensations she felt in *Gareth's* arms were a world apart from those she had experienced when hugging her cousin.

'Gareth—' she started to protest, but he was already dropping a light kiss on her forehead, and then a far less light, breathtakingly intimate and far too brief one on her startled parted lips.

'Goodnight,' he whispered against her mouth. 'Sleep well and don't worry... They'll both be safe with me and I'll bring them over in the morning.'

He had turned to go, marshalling the boys in front of him, before she could say or do anything.

Her hands, she discovered as she locked and barred the door after them, were trembling slightly, and her heart was racing as though she had just sprinted a hundred metres.

Why had he kissed her like that? Simply as an automatic reaction following the boys' example? But *his* kiss had not been... His kiss. His *kiss*. She closed her eyes and felt her face start to burn.

In the sitting room her telephone had started to ring. Quickly she pushed the memory of Gareth and the unexpected, heart-jerking, sweet tenderness of his brief kiss out of her mind, and went to answer its summons.

CHAPTER EIGHT

'Lou, it's me,' Louise heard Olivia announce herself. 'Your mother's told me what's happened. Where are the boys now? Are they…?'

'Gareth has taken them back to his flat with him for the night. I don't know whether or not Mum mentioned to you that he's working here in Brussels now, and—'

'Yes, yes, she did.' Olivia interrupted her quickly. Louise knew that Olivia would have remembered Gareth from Tuscany, and guessed that her cousin was far more anxious to talk about her brother than to discuss past acquaintanceships. She knew that she was right when Olivia cut across her to ask her worriedly, 'Lou, how is Jack? Is he…?'

'He *seems* fine,' Louise told her cautiously. 'He was sick after the travelling, but he's over that now, and he seemed chirpy enough this evening. The four of us went out for a meal—my apartment isn't really equipped for any serious cooking, but…' She hesitated.

'But what?' Olivia pressed her.

'Well, he *seems* okay, Livvy, but, easy as it would be to put all the blame for his upset on Max's shoulders, I can't help thinking that there's more to the situation than that. Jack is a sensible enough boy. He knows how Max is, and he knows as well how much my parents love him. I can't help wondering if this

159

desire to find your father is perhaps something he's been brooding on in secret for some time.'

'You've just put into words exactly what *I've* been thinking,' Olivia agreed. 'I feel *so* guilty, Lou. I should have seen...*guessed*. But I've been so tied up in my own life, the girls and Caspar. And Jack seemed so happy, and well adjusted to the fact that Dad and Mum were no longer on the scene, that I'm afraid I just assumed that he felt the same way about the situation as I do. But of course I was an adult when it all happened. Jack was only a child.'

Louise knew, without her cousin having to explain, what she meant by 'when it all happened'. She was referring to the disappearance of her father.

Louise's own father had tried to trace him, and so too had Olivia and Jack's mother, who was now divorced from him and remarried.

'Mmm... I was thinking about...everything...this evening while we were out,' Louise told her. 'Do you think, Livvy, that by trying to protect Jack from the truth we've perhaps made the situation more difficult for him to cope with? He's an intelligent boy, and from what Joss has let slip I get the impression that the pair of them have a pretty good idea of what actually happened. Of course your father's disappearance is bound to have left Jack with an awful lot of unanswered questions—and an increasing number of them, perhaps, as he grows up. After all, looking at it from Jack's point of view, he perhaps feels that when your father disappeared he took with him the answers...'

'You're very perceptive, Lou,' Olivia told her. 'I must admit I hadn't put myself in Jack's shoes and tried to see things from his point of view. When Dad took off, to be blunt, I was so shocked and traumatised by the discovery that he had virtually stolen someone else's money that I was glad he'd disappeared. I don't know *how* I would have dealt with the situation if he hadn't... By going he relieved me of the necessity of having to do anything other than let your father and Aunt Ruth clear up the mess that he had left behind.'

'I think you're being too hard on yourself, Livvy,' Louise protested. 'I don't know how I would have coped in your shoes. I have to admit that I can't help sympathising with Jack, though. I know that *this* time we've managed to nip his plans in the bud, but—'

'But what happens next?' Olivia interrupted her wryly. 'That's what's been worrying me...'

'Well, I've had a thought,' Louise began hesitantly. 'And it *is* only a thought, that's all...'

'Go on,' Olivia commanded.

'Well, perhaps if Jack felt less isolated, if my father could involve him in his own enquiries to try and locate your father... If Jack could be *involved*, somehow, that might at least stop him from bunking off school and help him to feel he has some say, some control in things.'

'I hear what you're saying,' Olivia told her. 'And, yes, I think you could be right. I'll talk to your father about it, *and* to Jack. Which reminds me. The reason I'm ringing is to tell you that Saul will be flying over to collect both boys. He was due to come over on business anyway, apparently, and he says it's no trouble for him to bring Joss and Jack back with him.'

'What...when will he be arriving?' Louise asked her quietly.

'He's advanced his meeting and he's leaving first

thing in the morning; he says his business should be over by mid-afternoon. Look, I must go; I can hear Alex crying. Thanks again, Lou…I'm *so* grateful to you. It was such a shock when your mother rang to tell me what had happened.'

'I know what you mean.'

Olivia paused. 'Lou, it won't be a *problem*, Saul coming to collect the boys, will it?' she asked tentatively.

'Not in the least,' Louise replied promptly and truthfully—meaning it.

'No…that's what Tullah said,' Olivia agreed after another small pause, and Louise knew that it was a measure of how far she had come that she felt not the least degree of chagrin or resentment at the thought of her cousin and Saul's wife discussing her.

Another measure of her maturity, she acknowledged with far less pleasure, was that she did not have the least inclination to confide to Olivia just *why* it was that she knew so positively that her feelings for Saul were no more than those of a cousin—and had been for a very long time. Since Tuscany, in fact…

Louise opened her eyes abruptly. She had been asleep, dreaming about Gareth. In her dream she had been trying to reach out towards him, to hold him and kiss him, but every time she'd tried to do so he'd moved away from her.

A glance at her alarm clock warned her that it would soon be time for her to get up. Not that she particularly *wanted* to go back to sleep. Not if she was going to have *those* kind of dreams.

After a quick breakfast, she rang her boss at home, explaining to her what had happened and asking if she might have the day off to look after the boys until Saul arrived to collect them.

'By all means,' Pam Carlisle assured her. 'How's the migraine, by the way?'

'Gone,' Louise told her. 'Fortunately.'

After she had finished talking to Pam she cleared away her breakfast things, wondering what time Gareth would bring the boys round, and what she was going to do with them until Saul arrived.

She had just finished tidying up the kitchen when she heard Gareth and the boys arrive. Going to the door to let them in, she was relieved to see that Jack was smiling.

'Thank you for giving them a bed for the night,' she said to Gareth as he followed them into her flat.

'I've been on the phone to the parents,' she informed both boys as she ushered them into her living room, a little disconcerted to realise that instead of leaving Gareth had closed the door and joined them. 'And Saul will be calling round later to take you both home.'

'Saul?' All three of them repeated his name with varying degrees of emotion, but it was Gareth's quick, sharp demand that overrode the other voices as they made eye contact and she saw the critical condemnation in his look.

She could see that Jack was beginning to look slightly uneasy, and quickly she reassured him.

'It's all right Jack,' she told him. 'Mum and Dad *do* understand. You should have told them that you wanted to find your father,' she pointed out gently to him, and when she saw that he might still be determined to head off for Spain, added, 'And maybe Dad has been a little at fault in neglecting to keep you

informed of...things. He *has* tried to find your father,
you know, and—'

'Is it true that Dad will have to go to prison if he
comes back to England?' Jack blurted out, his face
going scarlet as he focused anxiously on Louise.

'Who on earth told you that?' Louise asked him,
shocked.

Jack shook his head.

'No one...at least not in so many words. But
Max...'

'Max is a trouble-maker. He's like—'

'Like my father,' Jack interrupted her.

Louise bit her lip in consternation. Gareth was still
there and showed no sign of planning to leave, but
this was not a conversation she particularly wanted to
have with him as an observer—a critical observer, no
doubt, she decided irritably.

'So far as I know, Jack, your father *has* never been,
was never motivated by malice, which I have to be
honest and admit Max very often is. But it's true that
your father and Max do share certain personality
traits...'

'Uncle Jon once told me that the reason Dad was
the way he was is because...because Gramps spoiled
him...' Jack told her uncertainly.

'Gramps *did* spoil him,' Louise agreed. '*And* he has
spoiled Max too...given him...given them both the
impression that they have the right to put themselves
first.'

'Uncle Jon told me as well that no one should
blame Dad completely, because Gramps' expectations
of him had put him under a lot of pressure...'

'Yes, Gramps does have very, very high expectations of his favourites,' Louise agreed dryly.

'Dad can't have loved *us* very much, me and Livvy, can he?' Jack asked her huskily. 'Not and have done what he did. Uncle Jon would *never* disappear and leave all of you...'

'I'm sure that he *does* love you, Jack,' Louise contradicted him. 'The fact that he disappeared isn't a reflection on you, you know, and it *certainly* doesn't mean he doesn't *love* you. In fact, I expect that one of the reasons he left was because he *does* love you both, very, very much.'

She saw the look that Jack was giving her, and explained quietly, 'By leaving, he probably thought that he was helping to protect you.'

'Do you really think so?' Jack questioned her uncertainly.

'I'm sure of it,' Louise confirmed, sure now that Jack would return to Haslewich, and the loving family awaiting him.

'What time's Saul arriving?' Joss interrupted.

'He has some business, which will take him until after lunch, so I doubt that he will be here until late afternoon,' Louise informed him. 'Is there anything that either of you would like to see or do while you're here? I've taken the day off work so...'

'Gareth's going to take us to this place where we can surf the net,' Joss informed her excitedly.

Louise opened her mouth to point out that Gareth had no right to make any such arrangements without checking with her first that it was all right, and then closed it again.

'You can come with us if you want to. Can't she, Gareth?' Joss added.

'Gee, thanks,' Louise drawled as she looked across at Gareth, half expecting to see him sharing her amusement that Joss should think she might consider this a high treat.

But instead of smiling Gareth was frowning, his voice curt and terse as he demanded, 'I take it it was *your* idea that Saul should be the one to come for the boys?'

Louise looked at him.

'No, as a matter of fact, it wasn't—' she began.

But before she could finish he cut across her and said sarcastically, 'I see. So it was just a fortunate coincidence, was it?'

Louise looked across to where Joss and Jack were too deep in a highly technical discussion about some new computer technology to be aware of what was going on between Gareth and herself.

'I don't know *what* you're trying to imply,' she began in a heated, low-pitched voice, 'but for your information Saul is—'

'I know *exactly* what Saul is to you,' Gareth interrupted her savagely. 'My God, haven't you—?'

He stopped abruptly as Joss looked across at them both questioningly.

'I'd better get my coat,' Louise informed Gareth. 'How far is this place? Can we walk, or…?'

'No. I'll drive us there in my car,' Gareth informed her brusquely.

'If you've both finished, I think we ought to be heading back to the flat,' Louise informed Joss and Jack as she glanced quickly at her watch. Gareth had insisted on taking them for a late lunch at a small trattoria close to where they had spent the morning, and now, as they all stood up, Louise gave him a dismissive smile and told him, 'There's no need for you to drive us back. I'll get a taxi.'

All day she had been conscious of a very definite brooding hostility in his attitude towards her, and despite her determination not to let either him or the boys see how much it was affecting her the strain was beginning to take its toll.

She already knew, of course, that he neither liked nor approved of her, but the contempt she could feel emanating from him today had brought home to her just how very vulnerable she was where he was concerned.

'We can't go home without going to Gareth's flat to collect our stuff,' Joss reminded her practically.

Louise's heart sank. But he was right, of course. However, when they arrived at the apartment block, a little to Louise's consternation they discovered that Saul was already waiting in the foyer for them.

'Saul, I'm so sorry,' she apologised. 'I didn't think you'd be here until later.'

'Don't worry,' Saul reassured her as he smiled at her, and then looked thoughtfully towards Gareth. 'My business was completed earlier than I expected.'

'You must be Gareth.' Saul smiled, extending his hand towards the other man. 'I'm Saul Crighton, Louise's cousin...'

'And ours,' Joss added.

'Yes, I know,' Gareth acknowledged tersely, ignoring Saul's outstretched hand and turning instead to the two boys, reminding them, 'Your things are still in my apartment. I'll—'

'Oh, yes. You'd better go with Gareth now and get them,' Louise interrupted him quickly, seizing the opportunity to ensure that she had a few moments of privacy with Saul to put him fully in the picture just in case Olivia hadn't already done so.

Over the boys' heads Gareth sent her a corrosively contemptuous look. Her face burning, as much with unhappiness as anger, Louise looked away from him.

'Not exactly the friendly type, is he?' Saul commented dryly once he and Louise were on their own.

'You mean Gareth?' Louise asked, fumbling with the key as she started to unlock her apartment door. 'It's my fault… He… I…'

She stopped.

'He thinks I'm trying to manipulate the situation so that I can have some time on my own with you,' she told Saul with painful honesty as she pushed open her apartment door and beckoned to him to follow her inside.

'He…he was my tutor that time when…the time of the masked ball, and…' She stopped. 'In a way he's right I *did* want to have some time on my own with you, but not for the reason he suspects. I wanted to have a private word with you about Jack, Saul. I don't know how much Livvy has told you.'

'Not much at all…only that Jack has taken it into his head that he wants to find David.'

'Yes, that's right, he does. I've tried to talk to him, but I'm worried about him, and I wondered if perhaps you… He *needs* someone to confide in, someone he can talk to who he can trust.'

'I'll do my best,' Saul promised her gravely.

'He thinks his father didn't love him.'

Saul was starting to frown, and to her chagrin Louise suddenly felt her eyes fill with tears.

When he saw them Saul's frown deepened with concern.

'Lou...' he began. But she shook her head trying to smile as she told him huskily, 'Saul, I'm sorry... It's just... I can't understand why I'm such a fool. You'd think after the lessons I learned through having that fearsome crush on you that I'd know better than to risk loving a man who doesn't love me back. But...'

'A man who doesn't love you back... Are we talking about your extremely unfriendly friend and ex-tutor Gareth Simmonds, here?' Saul asked her dryly.

Louise shook her head, but it was no use; the strain of the last twenty-four hours was having its effect on her, and the next thing she knew she was in Saul's arms, her head pressed firmly against his shoulder while he comforted her in much the same way he had done many years ago, when she had still been a child suffering from the pain of a scraped knee. But broken skin could in no way be compared to the agony of a broken heart, and she wasn't a child any more but a woman, Louise reminded herself.

'I'm being an idiot. I'm sorry,' she apologised, blowing her nose firmly on the handkerchief he proffered as she gave him a frail smile.

She was still smiling up at him, and still held securely in his arms, several seconds later as the sitting-room door burst open and Joss and Jack, followed by Gareth, came in.

The sight of Louise in Saul's arms was plainly of no interest to either Joss or Jack, both of whom, in their different ways, were anticipating their return journey to Britain in Saul's charge with a certain amount of trepidation.

Gareth, though, reacted completely differently, coming to an abrupt halt only feet away from them and saying with open contempt, 'I'm sorry if we're interrupting something…private.'

Automatically Louise started to move away from Saul, but to her consternation, instead of letting her go, Saul kept a firm hold on her arm, his other hand giving her a small warning pinch out of Gareth's sight as he countered dangerously, 'Yes, so am I.' He turned his back on Gareth, so that his view of Louise's face was blocked as he told her tenderly, 'I meant what I said the last time we met, you know. You'll always be very…special to me, Lou…'

Louise gawped at him. What on earth was Saul trying to do? He must know the interpretation that Gareth would put on his comments after what she had just told him, and now here he was, quite deliberately, or so it seemed, adding some volatile and combustible material to the flames fuelling Gareth's suspicions.

'Come on, you two,' he instructed the boys, in a much firmer tone of voice, before turning to Gareth and telling him formally, 'It seems I owe you a debt of thanks…' And then, to Louise's bemusement, he lifted her hand to his mouth and gently kissed her fingers, before very firmly and expertly drawing her into his arms and holding her there intimately for a few long seconds.

Louise didn't offer to go down to the foyer to see Saul and the boys off; her legs felt as though they wouldn't carry her as far as her own front door, never mind the foyer.

What on *earth* had got into Saul to make him behave so…so outrageously? It must have been as obvious to him as it had to her that Gareth was not in the least amused by his behaviour. Shakily she closed her eyes and put her hand on the back of her small sofa to steady herself as the apartment door banged shut behind them all.

CHAPTER NINE

'HAVE you gone completely out of your mind? He's
a married man, for God's sake, and no matter how
much he might feel like having a bit of sex on the
side with you, right now I'll bet that's *all* he's got on
his mind. Have you stopped to *think* that if he really
wanted you, if he *really* cared…if he *really* had the
least degree of respect or affection for you, he would
never…?'

'Gareth.' Weakly Louise opened her eyes. 'I
thought you'd gone. What…?'

'For God's sake, Louise. He *might* be your
cousin…you *might* still love him, but—'

Louise had had enough—more than enough.

'No, I don't,' she corrected Gareth flatly. 'Or at
least I don't love him in the way that *you're* trying to
imply. And even if I did…' She pushed her hand
tiredly into her hair.

'If you don't love him then what the hell were you
doing in his arms back there?' Gareth demanded furiously.

'He was just holding me…comforting me…'
Louise told him wearily.

'Comforting you? Oh, my God, now I've heard everything—'

'That's right,' Louise interrupted him. 'You *have*.
Or at least you've heard all you *are* going to hear and
if you want the truth, Gareth, what I've *heard* is too
much…much too much from *you*. I want you to

leave,' she told him. 'You have to leave,' she added
with quiet desperation. 'You have to leave, Gareth,
because if you don't…'

She stopped, unable to say any more as one bright
tear and then another filled her eyes and splashed
down onto the hand she had lifted to wipe it away.

'Oh, God, Louise, how *can* you love a man
who…?'

'Who doesn't love *me*?' Louise supplied for him,
when, instead of obeying her command, Gareth took
a determined step towards her.

'A man who isn't *worthy* of your love,' Gareth corrected her gruffly. 'I know how you feel about me,
Lou. I know how much you dislike and resent me…'

He stopped as Louise gave a small strangled yelp
of mingled pain and laughter deep in her throat.

'No, you don't,' she told him bravely. 'You don't
know how I feel at all…because if you did… Gareth,
please, I just can't *cope* with this. You *have* to leave,'
she begged him.

But inexplicably, instead of obeying her, he was
suddenly reaching out for her and taking hold of her
and telling her hoarsely, 'I may not know how *you*
feel, Lou, but I certainly know how *I* feel, and how
I've felt for one hell of a long time. It's tearing me
apart, thinking about you wasting your love, your life,
on someone who…on a man who… I *know* he's your
cousin but…'

'For the last time, Saul is *not* the man I love,'
Louise told him, her self-control finally deserting her.
'You are that man, Gareth. *You* are the man I love,
the only man I have *ever* properly loved, and the only
man I am *ever* likely to properly love. The reason Saul
was holding me in his arms when you and the boys

walked in was because I had just been telling him about you, and—'

'Gareth! Gareth! Let go of me,' Louise demanded breathlessly as she lifted her hands to push him firmly away from her.

But it was too late, and besides, Gareth quite obviously had absolutely no intention whatsoever of letting her go. Instead he was demanding thickly, 'Say that again… You love *me*…? When…? How long…? Why…?' he began, and then stopped, closing his eyes and taking deep breaths before muttering something under his breath that Louise couldn't quite catch.

When he opened his eyes Louise felt her heart lurch dangerously against her chest wall as she saw the way he was looking at her.

'We can *talk* later,' Gareth informed her softly, barely breathing the words so that she automatically had to move even closer to him to hear what he was saying.

'Right now there's something far more important I need to do…far more important and far, far more pleasurable…'

'Gareth…' Louise protested weakly, but it was too late. His mouth was already moving over hers and she was responding to him, her body melting against his as his mouth moved more determinedly over hers, his tongue tracing the shape of her lips and then gently probing them apart.

'No,' Louise whispered, but the word was more a soft sigh of pleasure than any kind of real denial.

It was the longest, sweetest, most loving, cherishing kiss she had ever known, Louise decided dreamily as Gareth continued to caress her lips, his hand cupping her face, stroking her skin, his heartbeat thudding fiercely beneath the hand she had originally lifted to fend him off and which had now stayed to curl possessively into the front of his shirt. She felt dizzy, light-headed almost, with a mixture of desire and disbelief, unable to comprehend properly that this was actually happening, that *she* was *here* in Gareth's arms, that *he* was holding her, kissing her, loving her, as though he actually meant it.

'Have you any idea just how much I've been wanting to do this?' he was whispering against her mouth. 'How much I've *ached* to touch you…kiss you…*love* you, Louise?'

'I thought you despised me…disliked me,' she whispered back.

'Despised *myself*, disliked *myself*, yes. But *never* you,' Gareth groaned. 'When I came to the villa that morning…the morning after and found that you'd all left…I thought at first that it was because…that I'd…that you'd been so affected by what had happened, that your parents… But then Maria told me that there was some problem at home.'

'I *was* affected by what…what we did. But not in the way you mean,' Louise told him truthfully, shivering in delicious pleasure as his lips started to caress the soft curve of her throat.

'I knew that I'd…enjoyed…what happened, and that you'd made me feel things…do things…I'd no idea I could feel or do. But it wasn't until the following Christmas that I realised what had happened to me. I'd told myself that I hated you, that I was glad you weren't my tutor any longer and that there was no contact between us. I even managed to persuade myself that I was still in love with Saul, that I had simply transferred what I felt for him into a physical response to you…'

'Well, you certainly had *me* convinced,' Gareth interrupted her hoarsely. 'You called out his name when I…'

'I didn't even know I had…it must have been a protective reflex,' Louise told him softly, achingly. 'A way of trying to pretend to myself that you weren't…that I wasn't…' She stopped, and her eyes widened in fierce response as he ran his fingertip around the neckline of her top and her breasts immediately started to ache wantonly for his touch.

'Last time, when I went home, Saul and Tullah were both there. Everyone was tiptoeing around me as though I was an unexploded bomb. I admit I had been dreading seeing them myself, but when I did…' She looked up into his eyes. 'He was just Saul again,' she told him simply. 'Just my cousin. There was *nothing* else, and I couldn't really understand how I had ever thought…felt…wanted…

'Ever since Tuscany I have been having these dreams about you… Dreams when I…we… I thought it was simply because you were the one who…' She paused, flushing, and then laughing as she shook her head. 'I was so naive…naive and stubborn. I didn't *want* to admit the truth to myself, but I looked at Saul and I ached for you so badly…wanted you so badly…'

As her eyes filled with tears at the memory of the shocking fierceness of the pain, Gareth's eyes darkened in protective love.

'I was thinking about *you* as well,' he assured her. 'Wondering what you were doing…and who you were with…wishing it was me and wishing to hell that I hadn't been stupid enough to give way to feelings that I knew then were dangerous...'

'But you didn't *love* me when we...when you... You didn't *love* me. Not then,' Louise protested.

Gareth looked steadily at her.

'You're right. You *were* naive,' he told her huskily. 'Of course I damned well loved you. You don't think for a single solitary moment that I would actually have...that a man who didn't love...? You couldn't really have believed I could be so unprincipled as to...?'

'I thought you did it because you were angry with me,' Louise told him simply. 'I thought it must be a male reaction thing.'

'"A male reaction thing."' Gareth laughed huskily and closed his eyes. 'Oh, it was certainly that, all right,' he assured her. 'A *very* male reaction thing. The kind of male reaction thing that happens when a male, a *man*, falls deeply and passionately in love.

'I could have killed you when you told me that you were planning to lose your virginity with Giovanni. Do you know that?' he asked her lovingly.

'Well, you certainly made it plain that you didn't think it was a very good idea,' Louise agreed demurely. '*When* did you fall in love with me...?'

'It started one afternoon in my rooms. You were arguing passionately about something. I can't remember what. I looked at you and suddenly...' He paused and shook his head. 'It just happened. I told myself not to be a fool. I even reminded myself of all the reasons why it wouldn't work. And then you started skipping lectures, getting Katie to sit in for you instead...'

'Katie *said* you knew about that.'

'Of course I knew,' he told her lovingly, adding wryly, 'And so, too, did my body. It never reacted to Katie the way it did to you. And then, when I found out that you were in love with someone else…' He paused and shook his head. 'That day when I came to your room and found you there half-drunk…'

'I felt so humiliated that you'd seen me like that,' Louise whispered. 'And then you turned up in Tuscany…'

'I wasn't too pleased either. I'd gone there hoping to get things in perspective, to get my emotions under control, and instead…'

'Why didn't you *say* something…tell me how you felt?' Louise asked him.

'How *could* I when you'd already told me that the only man you could ever love was your precious Saul?'

'I knew in Tuscany that it was just a silly crush that had burned itself out, but I'd made such a big drama out of it that I couldn't bring myself to let it go. And then you took me to bed and I realised that you were right…that I had just been a girl…but after our afternoon together I woke up a woman, and it was as a woman that I began to realise that I loved you,' Louise told him softly.

'I couldn't repeat all the mistakes I'd made with Saul…I couldn't embarrass you and humiliate myself by putting you through all the stupid things I'd done to try and get Saul's attention—I didn't even *want* to. I could see just how ridiculous…how selfish and, yes, childish in many ways my behaviour had been. I knew then how different real adult love was from my teenage fantasy of what love was, which I had woven around my feelings for Saul.

I'd believed that if I just tried hard enough I could *make* Saul love me. With you… With you I *knew* that the only way your love could be mine was if you gave it to me freely, and I knew you would never do that…'

'You knew wrong, then, because you already had it,' Gareth whispered rawly to her. 'Oh, Lou, when I think of the time we've wasted, the days, the years, the nights we've spent apart when we could have been together.'

'Especially the nights,' Louise agreed wickedly, her mouth curling up at the corners, but she still blushed a little bit as she saw the way he was looking at her.

'It's been a long time,' he told her huskily. 'And there hasn't been anyone else for me since then, Louise…'

'There hasn't been anyone else for me either,' Louise told him a little shyly, adding shakily, 'What you…what we did…the way I felt, was so…so good…so right…that I couldn't…I didn't… I was afraid of spoiling the memory of it, because I knew no one else could ever make me feel the way you had done.'

'No one else?' Gareth quizzed her gently. 'Not even Jean Claude…?'

Louise burst out laughing.

'No one else,' she confided. 'And *especially* not Jean Claude…'

'Gareth, what is it? What are you doing?' she demanded as he suddenly turned away from her and reached for the telephone, quickly pushing the buttons and wrapping his free arm around her to stop her from moving away from him as he started to speak into the receiver.

'Paul, it's Gareth Simmonds here. Look, I'm not going to be around for the next few days—an urgent family matter... Yes... Well, the committee doesn't have another meeting until next month, I know... Can you check through my diary and cancel all my appointments for the next week, please? Oh, and by the way, can you ring the airport and book me two seats on the first available flight for Pisa? You can ring me back on this number,' he added quickly, giving Louise's telephone number and then replacing the receiver before she could say a word.

'Tuscany,' she said, her eyes starting to shine.

'Tuscany,' he agreed.

'But Pam...'

'No buts. Pam will be able to manage without you for a couple of days.' Gareth informed her masterfully, and then groaned as he added ruefully, 'I'm not quite sure how *I'm* going to manage to keep my hands off you until we reach the villa... You do realise, don't you, that it's a good two-hour drive from the airport and—?'

'The *villa*... But it might not be empty, and you could—'

'If it isn't empty then I shall bribe whoever is staying there to move out,' Gareth informed her determinedly. 'And besides...*my* family's villa *is* empty at the moment. It might not be quite the same—'

'*Your* family's villa? With the pool...' Louise interrupted him. 'The pool where I saw you swimming that day the Fiat broke down...?'

'Uh-huh...the very same one.'

Louise closed her eyes and gave a small, femininely ecstatic sigh.

'I want to go *there*,' she told him happily. 'Oh, yes,

I want to go *there*, Gareth. I want it to be
there…please…'

'Of course… But why…?'

A small smile curved her mouth as, leaning forward, she whispered to him, 'Because that's where I
realised for the first time just what a very, very sexy
man you are, and that's where, when I saw you getting out of the pool in those trunks, I couldn't help
wondering just how you'd look without them, and
that's where…'

'Okay, I think I get your drift,' Gareth told her
softly.

'Well…?' Gareth asked Louise lazily, smiling sexily
at her as he leaned over her sun lounger to kiss her
awake.

'Well, what?' she asked him, sitting up and taking
the drink he had brought her.

They had arrived at the villa in the early hours of
the previous morning. Louise had wanted to go
straight to bed, but Gareth had demurred.

'Let's wait until this afternoon,' he had suggested
meaningfully, and, her stomach knotting with sharp,
sensual excitement, Louise had agreed.

It…*he*…had been worth waiting for…*more* than
worth waiting for, and today her body still felt relaxed
and softly heavy with sensual satisfaction.

'Well, do I look just as good without my shorts as
you hoped?' Gareth teased her.

Louise laughed.

Last night Gareth had persuaded her to go skinny-
dipping with him, and afterwards they had made love
beside the pool in a tangle of damp limbs and soft,
warm towels.

'Oh, every bit as good...' she confirmed. 'But you can always prove it to me again if you want to,' she teased him provocatively.

'Oh, I *want* to,' Gareth assured her.

'I hope everything is going to work out all right for Jack,' Louise murmured, her eyes darkening a little as she thought about her young cousin. 'I feel that we've *all* been guilty of not realising how much his father's disappearance has affected him.'

'It *must* have been difficult for him,' Gareth agreed sombrely. 'But you handled the whole situation very well. You're going to be a very good mother, Lou...'

'But not yet,' she told him. 'Or at least not until we're married...'

'No, not until we're married. You'll make a lovely winter bride with your colouring...'

'A winter wedding...' Louise murmured.

'I have to warn you that I have at least a dozen nieces who will all want to be bridesmaids...'

Louise giggled. 'Oh, not a dozen, surely!'

'Well, four,' Gareth amended. 'You *do* want to marry me, don't you, Lou?' he asked her, his face and voice suddenly very serious.

'Oh, yes,' Louise assured him huskily. 'Oh, yes, Gareth. Yes...yes...yes...' she moaned, as his mouth covered hers and the sun lounger rocked perilously beneath their combined weight.

'Louise is going to marry Gareth Simmonds,' Joss informed his great-aunt Ruth solemnly as he sat in her drawing room eating the fresh scones she had just baked.

'So I understand,' she agreed, smiling over his head at her American husband, Grant. They had only been married a few years themselves, even if their love went back over several decades.

'I like him. He understands things...' Joss told them seriously. 'Maddy was crying again yesterday, when I went to see Gramps. Why does Max have to be so horrid to her?'

Ruth sighed as she looked at him.

'I'm afraid that Max is just like that, Joss,' she informed her great-nephew sadly. 'Some people are, and when they are I'm afraid it takes a miracle to change them.'

'But miracles do happen,' Joss pointed out gravely. 'Look at you and Uncle Grant.'

'They do, yes,' Ruth agreed.

'I hope one does happen to Max...for Maddy's sake,' Joss added.

Ruth looked at him calmly.

'I shouldn't build your hopes on it, Joss,' she warned him. 'Not where Max is concerned.'

'I still can't totally believe it,' Katie told her twin, shaking her head slightly. 'You and Gareth in love and getting married...'

'What Mum finds harder to believe is that I'm going for the whole traditional wedding bit, complete with dress and bridesmaids,' Louise informed her sister wryly. 'We're getting married Christmas week, and spending Christmas Day at home with the family. Then New Year in Scotland, with Gareth's family, before we go off on honeymoon.'

Katie was in Brussels with Louise, and Gareth had promised to take them both out for dinner.

'You like his family, then?' Katie asked her twin.

'Oh, yes,' Louise confirmed enthusiastically. 'A

small part of *me* still can't quite believe it, either, Katie, I feel so…so special…so…so lucky… so…'

'So loved?' Katie suggested gravely.

Louise frowned. Was that a small shadow she could hear in her twin's voice, see in her eyes, and, if so, why?

'Katie…' she began, but her sister was already getting to her feet and picking up their empty wine glasses.

'It's six o'clock,' she warned Louise. 'We're going to have to start making a move if we're to be ready for Gareth when he calls for us at seven-thirty.'

'You are going to be there, aren't you?' Louise demanded as she followed her into the kitchen. 'At the wedding, I mean… No last-minute trips to the back of beyond to inspect some irrigation scheme or anything…'

'It's documents that I inspect, Lou, not irrigation schemes,' Katie reminded her lightly. 'And, yes, I shall be there.'

She was glad that she had been alone when she had taken Louise's ecstatic telephone call to tell her that she and Gareth were going to be married. Louise had put her silence down to the fact that she had been so surprised by her news… Well, she *had* been surprised, but…

Louise wasn't the only one who could love inappropriately and unwontedly. Not that Katie had ever imagined that Gareth might feel something for *her*, but then neither had she suspected that he was actually in love with her twin.

Anyway, whatever foolish dreams she might once have had had been packed away quietly and for ever now, along with all the other things that belonged to her childhood and the past. And, yes, of course she would be at their wedding, and she would smile for them and *with* them. How could she not? How could she not be happy for her twin? And how could she not grieve a little for herself?

'We'll never be alone, Katie,' Louise had once told her. 'We'll *always* have each other.'

But Louise had been wrong and now she *was* alone. Alone and lonely and hurting.

'You know that Gareth actually knew right from the start when you attended his lectures in my place that you weren't me?' Louise burbled happily as Katie quietly washed her used glass. 'He could tell the difference between us because he loved me...'

'Yes, you told me,' Katie acknowledged calmly, her hand trembling a little as she put the clean glass down.

'I love him so much, Katie,' Louise told her sister softly. 'I just wish that you... I want you to be as happy as I am...I want you to have someone to love and be loved by.'

'I'm happy as I am,' Katie told her, and promised herself that one day, very soon, it would be true.

* * * * *

Read on for a tantalising extract from Penny Jordan's next book, which features Max and Maddy Crighton's story.

THE PERFECT SINNER

Available soon from MIRA® Books

CHAPTER ONE

'DADDY,' Max heard Leo breathe blissfully as he burrowed as close to him as he could get. And then more shakily, 'Daddy,' before Max turned his head and kissed him.

To Jenny, who had planned to keep the children out of Max's way until she had ascertained his mood, her initial emotion on discovering that the children had left the kitchen where she had told them to stay and were in the hall, was one of trepidation. So the sight of Max kneeling down on the floor, his arms wrapped around Leo's small body as he cradled him lovingly in his arms before lifting his head and extending one open arm to Emma, who was watching with her mouth open and her eyes rounding, was one that shocked Jenny so much that she could only stare at the small tableau in mute disbelief.

Maddy could see Max standing up. She was too shocked to register or analyze the sound of his voice as he called her name and took a step towards her, Emma in his arms and Leo clinging determinedly to his side.

Maddy was aware of the expectant look in Jenny's eyes as he turned towards his wife, but it was impossible for Maddy to respond, to reciprocate the warmth she could see in Max's eyes, to play the part she could sense that everyone was willing her to play in his homecoming and, instead of answering him, she

turned swiftly on her heel and almost ran the length
of the hall before disappearing into the kitchen.

Before the kitchen door closed behind her she could
hear Leo asking shakily in the silence she had left
behind, 'Where has Mummy gone?'

'I expect she's gone to put the kettle on,' Max comforted Leo gently, but his head was bent over Emma's
so that neither of his parents nor his grandfather could
see his expression.

It had been a shock to see Maddy and, for a moment, when she had first walked into the hall, even
though he had known that it *was* her, visually his eyes
had almost refused to recognise his wife.

She had lost weight, her hair done in a different
style, but those things alone weren't responsible for
the change he had immediately sensed in her. There
was a new determination about her, a new strength, a
resistance to him, which he had felt as strongly as
though she had physically pushed him away. But
more than all of those things, what had shocked and
disturbed him even more had been his own reaction
to her.

In place of the regret and indifference he had expected to feel, his body was reacting as though he
wanted to pick her up and carry her up those stairs in
front of him...

HARLEQUIN PRESENTS®

Wedded Bliss

Penny Jordan   Carole Mortimer

Two brand-new stories—for the price of one!—
in one easy-to-read volume.
Especially written by your favorite authors!

Wedded Bliss
Harlequin Presents #2031, June 1999
THEY'RE WED AGAIN!
by Penny Jordan
and
THE MAN SHE'LL MARRY
by Carole Mortimer

There's nothing more exciting than a wedding!
Share the excitement as two couples make their very
different journeys which will take them up the aisle to
embark upon a life of happiness!

Available **next month** wherever Harlequin books
are sold.

HARLEQUIN®
Makes any time special ™

Coming Next Month

HARLEQUIN PRESENTS®

THE BEST HAS JUST GOTTEN BETTER!